"It's going to be all right. I promise."

His words got to her. They made her feel defenseless and vulnerable. And yet, at the same time, they made her feel safe because he understood, maybe better than she did, what she was going through at the moment.

She clung to him, trying to hang on to his strength, trying desperately to get her own back.

Looking back later, Olivia wouldn't be able to say with any certainty just what steps came next and who was responsible.

One moment, she was crying her heart out, damning her poor self-control for breaking down this way. The next moment, she'd turned up her face to his and found herself kissing him.

Dear Reader,

This is actually my second book for Harlequin American Romance. My first came out in April of 1986. A great deal has happened since then, both to me and to the line. Happily, we've both done well and thrived.

What you have before you is my first venture into the small, neighborly town of Forever, Texas. The sheriff there, Enrique Santiago, is half Black Irish on his mother's side, one quarter Apache and one quarter Latino on his father's side and a complete tall, dark and handsome hunk. But Dallas trial lawyer Olivia Blayne isn't looking for a hunk when she blows into town. She's searching for her infant nephew, Bobby, and her runaway sister, Tina. Rick helps her on her journey and, along the way, these two people from two different worlds find themselves, each other—and love.

I hope you find that you enjoy your visit to Forever because the town has other stories to tell and I'd more than welcome having a friendly face in the audience.

As ever, I thank you for reading and, from the bottom of my heart, I wish you someone to love who loves you back.

Marie Ferrarella

Marie Ferrarella

THE SHERIFF'S CHRISTMAS SURPRISE

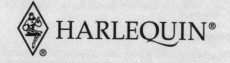

HARLEQUIN®

TORONTO • NEW YORK • LONDON
AMSTERDAM • PARIS • SYDNEY • HAMBURG
STOCKHOLM • ATHENS • TOKYO • MILAN • MADRID
PRAGUE • WARSAW • BUDAPEST • AUCKLAND

Recycling programs
for this product may
not exist in your area.

ISBN-13: 978-0-373-75333-8

THE SHERIFF'S CHRISTMAS SURPRISE

ABOUT THE AUTHOR

Marie Ferrarella is a *USA TODAY* bestselling and RITA®
Award-winning author who has written more than two
hundred books for Silhouette and Harlequin Books,
some under the name of Marie Nicole. Her romances
are beloved by fans worldwide. Visit her website at
www.marieferrarella.com.

Books by Marie Ferrarella

Chapter One

It was a nice little town, as far as relatively small towns went. Hardly any trouble at all.

Which, when he came right down to it, was the problem. The town was nice; it was little and it was peaceful.

And Sheriff Enrique Santiago was restless.

Rick's people had lived in and around Forever, Texas, as far back as anyone could remember. This was especially true of the Mexican and the Apache branches of his family. The Black Irish contingent came later, but still far back enough to be only slightly less old than the veritable hills.

All three branches had left their indelible mark on Rick, found in his gaunt cheekbones, his blue-black, thick straight hair and his exceedingly vivid green eyes, which could look right through a man's lies.

He was a walking embodiment of the nationalities that called Forever their home. But he wanted something different, something that would make his adrenaline accelerate, at least once in a while. The need to feel alive was why he'd taken the post of sheriff to begin with.

But being sheriff in Forever meant breaking up an

occasional fistfight when the weather was too hot and tempers were too short. It meant making sure Miss Irene wasn't wandering around town in the middle of the night in her nightgown, sleepwalking again. Or worse, driving through the center of town in her vintage Mustang while sound asleep.

It wasn't that he hankered after dead bodies piled up on top of each other, but he did yearn for days that weren't all stamped with a sameness that had the capacity to drive a sane man crazy.

And that was why these days he was thinking about moving north. Specifically, Dallas. Not just looking, but doing something about it. He had a friend on the Dallas police force, Sam Rogers, a born and bred native of Forever. Sam had let him know that the Dallas police force was hiring again. So he'd filled out an application and requested an interview.

And waited.

A Captain Amos Rutherford had called him Wednesday and told him that they liked what they read and were interested. The man promised to get back to him about a time and place that was convenient for them both for the interview.

The promise of an interview had put a bounce in his step this morning, the day after Thanksgiving. Never one to dawdle, he got ready even more quickly than usual. Moving fast, he threw open the front door and his size-eleven boot came a hairbreadth away from kicking what appeared to be an infant seat that was smack in the middle of his doorstep.

An occupied infant seat.

The occupant of the infant seat made a noise just

before the toe of Rick's boot made contact with said infant seat. His hands flying out to the doorjamb in an effort to keep from pitching forward, Rick managed to catch himself just in time.

"What the—?"

Stunned and surprised but ever mindful of the five-foot nothing, formidable grandmother who had raised him, Rick bit off the curse that shot to his lips. He gazed down at the infant seat and the baby he very nearly had wound up punting across his front yard.

As if sensing the attention, the infant, all waving arms and gurgling noises, swaddled in blue, looked right back up at him. Intense blue eyes met green.

The baby was smiling.

Rick was not.

This had to be somebody's really poor idea of a joke, Rick thought, although the point of it eluded him.

Immediately, his deputies came to mind. He'd said more than once that nothing ever happened in Forever and his three-man team, which contained one woman, had also heard him say more than once that he was seriously thinking about leaving the small town because the boredom was getting to him.

This was undoubtedly their idea of "excitement."

Rick glanced around the immediate vicinity. He lived approximately five miles out of town, on a small plot that was barely half an acre. The terrain was as flat as an opened bottle of last week's ginger ale and if there was someone hanging around to witness his immediate reaction to the baby, they would have been hard-pressed to find a hiding place.

There was no one around.

Rick frowned and squatted down to get a close look at the baby. It didn't help. He didn't recognize the infant.

With a sigh, he picked up the infant seat and rose to his feet.

The baby was blowing bubbles, drooling on everything and appeared unfazed by the fact that he was out here, apparently all by himself for who knew how long.

Rick touched the baby's hand to see if it was cold. The temperature had dropped down to the upper forties during the night. The tiny, curled fist was warm. The baby had to have been dropped off in the past hour.

He scanned the area again. Still no one.

Rick had always had an eye for detail and for faces. His only requirement was that the faces had to belong to someone who was at least two years old. Prior to that, one baby looked pretty much like another to him.

Which was why he didn't recognize the infant he was holding.

"This someone's idea of a joke?" he asked out loud, raising his voice.

Only the wind answered.

Holding the infant seat against him with one arm, Rick gingerly felt around the baby to see if a note had been left and slipped in between the baby and the seat. As he disturbed the blanket in his search, an overwhelming, pungent odor rose up.

"Oh, you've got to be kidding me," he muttered, his nose wrinkling automatically.

His uninvited visitor made another, louder grunting noise, doing away with any doubts about what was going on. There was a full diaper to be reckoned with.

"Okay, enough's enough," Rick called out. "Take your kid back."

But no one materialized. Whoever had dropped the child off on his doorstep was gone.

Rick's frown deepened. "You didn't come with your own set of diapers, did you?" The baby gurgled in response.

"Yeah, I didn't think so," Rick muttered, shaking his head. "Hope you like dish towels," he told the baby as he walked back into the house.

Rick knew without having to raid his medicine cabinet that he had no powder to use on the baby, but because his Mexican grandmother had been adamant about his learning how to cook when he was a boy, he knew he had cornstarch in the pantry. Cornstarch was fairly good at absorbing moisture.

"Beggars can't be choosers," he told the infant as he appropriated the box of cornstarch off the shelf.

With nothing faintly resembling a diaper and only one set of extra sheets, which he was *not* about to rip up, Rick was forced to press a couple of clean dish towels into service.

Armed with the towels and box of cornstarch, he laid the baby down on the kitchen table and proceeded to change him.

He had no problem with getting dirty and more than once had sunk his hands into mud when the situation called for it. But when it came to this task, he proceeded gingerly.

And with good reason.

When he opened the diaper, he almost stumbled backward.

"What are you, hollow?" he demanded, stunned at just how much of a "deposit" he found. "How can something so cute be so full of…that?" he asked.

The baby responded by trying to stuff both fists into his mouth.

He was hungry, Rick thought. "Well, no wonder you're hungry," he commented. "You emptied everything out." As quickly as possible, he got rid of the dirty diaper, cleaned up his tiny visitor and put on the clean, makeshift replacement. "Let's get you back to your mama," he told the baby, laying him back down into the infant seat and strapping him in.

Within five minutes, Rick was in his four-wheel-drive vehicle, his unwanted companion secured in the backseat, and on his way into town.

"YOU BROUGHT us something to eat?" Deputy Larry Conroy asked, perking up when he glanced toward the man who signed his paychecks as the latter came through the front door.

From where Conroy sat, he could see that the sheriff was carrying something. Given an appetite that never seemed to be sated, nine times out of ten, Larry's mind immediately went to thoughts of food.

"Not unless you're a cannibal," Alma Rodriguez commented, looking around Rick's arm and into the basket. "What a cute baby." She eyed her boss and asked, "Whose is it?"

Rick marched over to the desk closest to the door—it happened to belong to his third deputy, Joe Lone Wolf— and set the infant seat down.

Long, lean and lanky, Joe jumped to his feet and

looked down at the occupant of the infant seat as if he expected the baby to suddenly turn into a nest of snakes.

"I was just about to ask you three that," Rick answered, his glance sweeping over the deputies.

"Us?" Larry exchanged glances with the other two deputies, then looked back at his boss. "Why us? What do we have to do with it?" He nodded at the baby, who was obviously "it."

Hope dwindled that this was just a prank. "Because I figured that one of you left him on my doorstep."

Alma had a weakness for babies and a biological clock that was ticking louder and louder these days. She was making funny faces at the baby, trying to get the infant to laugh. "It's a he?" she asked.

"Well, yeah," Larry said, as if she should have figured that part out quickly. "He's wearing blue."

Joe slid back into his chair, pushing it slightly away from his desk and the baby on it. "Doesn't mean anything."

"It's a he," Rick confirmed, his tone indicating that the baby's gender was *not* the important issue. "And I want to know where he came from. Any of you ever seen him before?"

Forever had not yet cracked the thousand-occupant mark. Be that as it may, he wasn't familiar with everyone who called the small town home. In addition, Forever stood right in the path of a well-traveled highway and had more than its share of people passing through. For all he knew, this little guy belonged to someone who had made a pit stop in Forever for a meal and had gotten separated from his family for some reason.

Larry looked at the baby again and shook his head. "Nope, don't recognize him."

Joe had already scrutinized his temporary desktop ornament. "Never saw him before."

"How can you be so sure?" Rick asked. "They all look alike at this age."

"No, they don't," Alma protested. "Look at that personality. It's all over his face." She realized that the others were watching her as if she'd taken leave of her senses. "What? Just because you're all blind doesn't mean I have to be."

"So you recognize him?" Rick asked, relieved.

"I didn't say that," she countered. Turning back to the baby, she studied him one last time and then shook her head sadly. "No, I never saw him before. This baby's not from around Forever."

"You know every baby in Forever?" Larry asked skeptically.

"Pretty much," she answered matter-of-factly. "Hey, I'm a law enforcement officer. It's my job to notice things," she added defensively. Alma had to raise her voice to be heard above the baby, who had begun fussing. Loudly.

Joe looked at him. "I think the kid wants you to hold him."

"Since when did you become such an expert on babies?" Larry asked.

Wide shoulders rose and fell in a careless manner. "Just seemed logical, that's all," Joe responded.

"I'll hold him," Alma volunteered. But when she took the baby into her arms, he only cried louder.

Reluctantly, Rick took the baby from her. The infant instantly quieted down.

"Looks like you've got the knack, Sheriff," Larry chuckled.

If he had it, Rick thought, he didn't want it. People this small made him nervous. He could easily see himself dropping the baby.

"Why don't you take him to Miss Joan's?" Alma suggested. "Everyone who comes through town stops there to eat. Maybe she remembers seeing him with his parents."

"Or if he does belong to someone in town, she'd recognize him," Larry added, "just in case you *don't* know every kid in town, Alma."

Rick looked at his three deputies one by one, his deep green, penetrating eyes locking with each pair in turn. He knew them, knew their habits. Neither Larry nor Alma could maintain a straight face if this was a hoax. Joe, he wasn't so sure about.

But to his disappointment, not one of his deputies was grinning. Or looking guilty. This was on the level. Someone had left a baby on his doorstep.

Why?

Rick sighed, placed the baby back into the infant seat, strapped him in again and then picked up the infant seat. He looked down at the baby. The little boy was smiling again.

At least the kid had something to smile about, he thought.

"Anybody wants me," he murmured as he left, "I'll be at the diner."

JOAN RANDALL, fondly referred to as "Miss Joan" by everyone, had run the local diner for as long as anyone in town could remember. Five foot five, with rounded curves and hair that looked to be just a wee bit too strawberry in color, the years had been kind to her. For the most part, she'd kept the wrinkles at bay despite her advancing age. Her eyes were quick to smile and she had an earth-mother quality about her that coaxed complete strangers to suddenly open up and share their life stories with her.

She had the same effect on the people she rubbed elbows with on a daily basis.

Rick had once ventured that Miss Joan had heard more confessions than all the priests within a fifty-mile radius put together.

The older woman lit up when she saw Rick walk through the door, a fond smile growing fonder when she saw that he was not alone.

"Whatcha got there, Sheriff Santiago," she teased, coming around the counter to come closer to him. "A new deputy?"

"I was hoping you could tell me," Rick answered. He carefully placed the infant seat on top of the counter, making sure that the baby was secure and that the seat didn't wobble.

No longer being lulled by the soothing constant motion of Rick walking, the baby began to fuss and complain again.

Having come over on the other side of the counter, Miss Joan peered into the infant seat. She studied the infant for a moment, then raised her eyes to Rick's.

"Looks like the little guy who was in here yesterday," she told him.

"Do you remember what the people with him looked like?" Rick realized that the question had come out a bit testily. He was quick to apologize. "Sorry." He kept one hand on the infant seat; the other he dragged through his hair. "This hasn't exactly been one of my better mornings."

Miss Joan smiled understandingly, then her brown eyes shifted toward the baby.

"I'm sure this little guy could say the same thing." Leaning in closer, she cooed at the infant. "Where's your mama, honey?"

"You remember what his parents looked like?" Rick pressed again, hoping that he would be able to get to the bottom of this fairly soon.

If the boy's parents had really abandoned him, then there were consequences to face, but he was hoping a logical reason was behind this.

"I sure do, they were the only strangers here on Thanksgiving. They looked like two sticks," Miss Joan told him. "One thinner than the other." She frowned, recalling. "The guy hardly looked old enough to shave and he had one short temper. Kept complaining and telling the little bit of a thing with him to shut the baby up. The little guy kept fussing." She smiled as she nodded at the infant. "Like the way he is now."

"The baby's mama seemed kinda tense," Guadalupe Lopez, one of Miss Joan's three waitresses and the only one who worked part-time, volunteered as she set down the sugar dispenser she was refilling and crossed over to them. "I thought she was going to cry a couple of times.

I wanted to say something, but it wasn't my place. The customer's always right." She raised her eyes to her boss. "Right, Miss Joan?"

"Most of the time," Miss Joan amended. She turned her attention toward Rick. "I felt sorry for the baby and for his mama, but can't rightly say I was sorry to see them all go. That baby's daddy had a mean streak a mile wide. Didn't want any trouble—" Her knowing eyes shifted to Rick's face. "Unless it means that it would keep you hanging around here—and us—a little longer," Miss Joan said, looking at Rick significantly.

So what happened between yesterday and this morning to separate thin parents from chubby baby? Rick wondered. "Did you happen to see if his parents were leaving town or if they were visiting someone?"

"Looked as if they were headed out of Forever to me. I heard the guy saying something about wanting to burn rubber." Miss Joan slid her forefinger along the baby's cheek. Her smile deepened. "So where did you find this little guy?"

"On my doorstep."

The two women looked surprised. "Huh," Lupe uttered, looking amused. "Don't that beat all."

"Not hardly," Rick muttered. This didn't make any sense. He definitely didn't know anyone who resembled sticks. Why had they picked him to be the one they left their son with? Or had they picked him? Maybe it was just a random choice. "Look, I've got to go see if I can find these people and find out what the—" he glanced at the baby and switched words "—heck is going on. Would you look after him for me?"

He deliberately didn't address either woman, leaving

it up to them which one would say yes. When there was no immediate taker, he added, "I can't take him with me while I'm running down his parents. No telling how long I'll be out and I think the little guy's hungry."

The infant was back to shoving his fists into his mouth.

"I can see your point," Miss Joan agreed. She pursed her lips as she looked at the infant. "I've got a diner to run and I don't have much experience with short people." Her eyes shifted over to the petite waitress. Lupe came from a large family. Eleven kids in all and she was the oldest. "Don't you have a bunch of little brothers and sisters, Lupe?"

"Too many," Lupe said with a sigh. "Why? You want one?"

"No, but…" Miss Joan's voice trailed off, but her meaning was quite clear.

Lupe seemed to know better than to resist. Besides, it was obvious she thought the little guy was cute.

"I can take care of him for you, Sheriff," she volunteered. She turned the infant seat around toward her and began to unfasten the straps securing the baby. Freeing the infant, she picked him up. "But make sure you come back."

"Don't worry, I will," he promised. With that, he made his way to the door.

Rick was back faster than he intended.

Strictly speaking, he was back before he left. Opening the door, he was about to walk out of the diner when a statuesque blonde all but knocked him over. Contact was hard, jarring, and oddly electric as their bodies slammed together, then sprang apart.

Stunned, with some of the wind knocked out of her, the woman staggered, somehow managing to keep from falling, but just barely.

"I'm sorry, I didn't mean to run into you like that," she apologized in a deeply melodic voice that reminded him of aged whiskey sliding down the side of a thick glass on a chilled winter morning.

His badge and uniform seemed to register belatedly in her brain and she added, "But you're the man I need to see—" The baby made another noise, pulling her attention over to where Lupe stood holding the baby. Her eyes widened.

"Bobby!" she cried, appearing stunned and thrilled all at the same time.

Chapter Two

Trial attorney Olivia Blayne was seven steps beyond bone tired.

The twenty-nine-year-old had been on the road for more hours than she cared to think about, taking off the second she finally managed to get a lead on her younger sister's location. That was thanks to an ex-boyfriend who knew someone who could track down the coordinates of her last cell-phone call, a service which, ironically, she paid for.

In reality, she'd been paying for her sister since the day their parents had been killed, victims of a senseless robbery at the small jewelry store they owned and operated.

From the moment she'd left Dallas behind in her rearview mirror two days before Thanksgiving, Olivia had haunted every roadside diner from there to here—a small town two steps away from the border—in hopes of finding her sister and her three-month-old nephew, Bobby.

Ordinarily extremely law-abiding, she had driven like a woman possessed, determined to bring both of them back to Dallas—preferably over Don Norman's dead body, she thought bitterly.

But as the hours peeled away—and her stomach protested more frequently that she'd put off eating—Olivia started to despair that she was on a fool's errand and was never going to find either her sister or the baby.

Robert Blayne, her father and ever the pragmatic one, had taught her to rely on logic; Diana, her mother, to believe in miracles. In Olivia's estimation, she needed the latter, not the former. The former was far too daunting to think about now.

When she all but collided with the six-foot-something rugged officer in a khaki uniform, she found her miracle. Or at least half of it.

It took Olivia less than a second to recover and rush over to the young, fresh-faced Hispanic woman holding her nephew.

Her heart, all but bursting with joy, leaped into her throat.

"Bobby," she cried again, tears smarting her eyes. She blinked twice, refusing to let them escape. She'd always hated women who broke down and cried. Crying was a sign of weakness and she couldn't allow herself to be weak, not even for a moment. Far too much depended on her being strong.

Olivia stretched out her arms to the infant, eager to take him from the petite, dark-eyed waitress.

Hesitating, Lupe looked toward Rick for guidance and he nodded. Only then did she let the baby be taken from her by the woman in the deep blue—and somewhat dusty—power suit.

Bobby felt like heaven in her arms. For a second,

Olivia pressed her cheek against his, just savoring the moment, the contact.

"Oh, Bobby, I was beginning to think I'd never see you again," she whispered to him.

Bobby wriggled, making a noise and seeking freedom. Reluctantly, Olivia loosened her hold on him, resting him against her shoulder. She'd discovered that, at least for now, it was his favorite position.

"So 'Bobby' is yours?" In Rick's estimation, the question was a needless one, but he still had to ask it. There were rules to follow, even in a town as small and laid-back as Forever.

The question indicated that the sheriff thought Bobby was her son, so she said, "No." The second the word was out, she negated her response, afraid that the man might think she was just some crazy woman, jumping at the chance to grab a baby.

God knew she probably looked the part, she thought, catching a glimpse of her reflection in the aluminum-covered bread box.

"Yes."

The woman in the expensive suit looked just a bit flustered, her pinned-up hair coming loose in different sections. Rick allowed his amusement to show. "Is this like some kind of a Solomon thing?"

For a moment, Olivia didn't answer. She hadn't realized how good it would feel to have this little bundle of humanity in her arms again until she'd begun to believe that she never would.

"No." Swaying just a little to lull the baby, Olivia continued to hold him against her shoulder as she looked at the man with the rock-solid chest and the annoying questions. "Bobby's my nephew." One hand cupping the back of Bobby's downy head, she turned and scanned the all-but-empty diner. A sinking feeling was setting in again. Tina wasn't here. "Where's my sister?" she asked.

Rick had a question of his own for her. "I take it that's the baby's mother?"

At twenty-four, Tina had turned out to be much too young to be a mother. Or at least, much too immature. But, for better or for worse, Tina was still Bobby's mother.

"Yes."

Rick nodded, leaning back against the counter. "I was hoping *you* could tell me where she was."

Damn.

Olivia focused on the small-town sheriff for the first time, her eyebrows drawing together as she did a quick assessment of the man, a skill she found useful in the context of her present vocation. She could tell if a man was being sincere, or if he was lying. The only time her ability seemed to fail her was when it came to Tina. But maybe that was because the thought of her sister lying to her, after all that they'd been through, was particularly hurtful.

She wanted to believe that Tina was better than that. Wanted to, but really couldn't. Not any longer. Not after the disappearing act she'd pulled.

"Sheriff, I've been trying to find Tina and the lowlife who forced her to run off with him for the last forty-eight hours. All I know is that she should be somewhere around here."

As she spoke, Olivia became aware that the matronly

looking woman behind the counter, who was quite blatantly listening intently to every word, had placed a cup
of coffee and a powdered bun on a small plate practically directly in front of her.

Olivia raised her eyes to the woman's, an unspoken
question in them.

The woman was quick to smile. "Thought you might
need that right about now, honey," the older woman said.
"You look like you're running on empty."

Admitting a weakness, or even that she was human,
was not something Olivia did readily, even to someone
she'd never see again. But she had been turned so inside
out these past few days, what with one thing and another,
that the protest that quickly rose to her lips turned into
a simple "Thank you."

The next moment, giving in to her tightening stomach, she took a long sip of the inky coffee. And felt
human again. Almost.

Watching, Miss Joan slanted a quick look toward
Rick and then chuckled, pleased that, once again, her
intuition had been right.

"I was gonna ask if you wanted cream and sugar with
that, but I guess not."

"Better?" Rick asked the baby's aunt when she came
up for air and set down the cup.

Olivia nodded. "Better." Her eyes shifted toward the
woman behind the counter. "How much do I owe you?"
she asked, setting her purse on the counter and attempting to angle into it with one hand while still holding
Bobby.

Miss Joan waved away the gesture. "It's on the house,
honey." And then she winked. "It's my good deed for

the day. Everyone should do one good deed every day. World would be a whole lot nicer," she declared with a finality that left no invitation for debate.

Rick had waited patiently for the almost criminally attractive woman to finish her coffee. He figured it would help her pull herself together. He wasn't going anywhere and there was no hurry, but he did want some answers. Most of all, he wanted to know why the infant had been left on his doorstep. Was it happenstance, or was there some reason he'd been singled out?

"Is your sister an underage runaway?" he asked the baby's aunt.

Olivia sighed. "Tina's not underage, she's twenty-four and technically, she's not a runaway." She set her mouth hard as she thought of her sister's boyfriend. She had tried, really tried, to make him feel welcome—she should have had her head examined—and drop-kicked the jerk into the middle of next year. "He forced her to go with him."

Rick raised an eyebrow. First things first. "Who's *he?*"

Olivia laughed shortly. The sheriff had inadvertently echoed her own sentiments. Just who *was* the tall, gangly, brooding individual who looked like a poor, dark-haired version of a James Dean wannabe? Or maybe it was that new sensation, the actor who was playing a vampire, that Don fancied himself to resemble? Whoever Don Norman envisioned himself to be, he had managed to brainwash her sister, turning Tina into some kind of mindless lemming who would follow this worthless human being off the edge of a cliff.

Well, not while she was around, Olivia silently vowed.

Not while there was a breath left in her body. If she had to, she would drag Tina back kicking and screaming and sit on her sister until she came to her senses.

But none of this did she want to share with a virtual stranger no matter *how* good-looking he was. Her sister's insanely poor judgment was her business. It was *not* up for public scrutiny.

"*He* is Don Norman," she told the sheriff. The moment stretched out and she knew the man was waiting for more. "And ever since he came into my sister's life, Norman has turned it upside down, and turned my sister into some pathetic, mindless groupie."

"Groupie," Rick repeated. The word had a definite connotation. He made the only logical connection. "This Norman's a musician?"

Olivia laughed shortly again. Don thought of himself as a musician, but as far as she knew, he'd never gotten paid and was currently part of no band.

"Among other things, or so he says," she replied crisply. "Mostly he's just a waste of human skin." She looked down at the baby in her arms.

Please don't take after your father, she implored Bobby silently.

"Sounds like you don't like him much," Miss Joan speculated, wiping down the same spot on the counter that she'd been massaging for the past few minutes.

"No, that's not true. I don't like him *at all*," Olivia corrected. "I tried, for Tina's sake." She patted the baby's back, moving her hand in slow, small concentric circles. The repetitive movement tended to soothe him. "And for Bobby's. But it's really hard to like someone who repays you for putting him up for six months by stealing your jewelry."

"He stole your jewelry?" Rick asked, his interest in the case piquing. "You're sure that he was the one who took it and not—"

Olivia saw where the sheriff was going with this and cut him off.

"Tina didn't have to steal anything from me. All she had to do was ask and I'd give her whatever she needed. I *have* been giving her everything she's needed." Olivia pressed her lips together. *And how's that working out for you?* a voice in her head jeered. "Norman's the thief," Olivia insisted. "He stole the jewelry, he stole my sister. I don't care about the jewelry, that's replaceable," she told the sheriff, struggling to hold on to her temper. It wasn't easy. Just thinking of Don pushed all her buttons. "My sister is not. And I am really afraid that something terrible is going to happen to her if she stays with the man."

She raised her eyes to the sheriff's. It killed her to ask a stranger for help, but she knew when she was out of her element. Tina's welfare took precedence over her pride.

"Can you help me find them, Sheriff?"

He'd always been a fairly decent judge of character. He had a feeling that the woman before him was used to taking charge of a situation. Was this actually nothing more than a glorified matter of power play? Did she resent the fact that her sister had run off with a boyfriend she disapproved of?

"If your sister left with this Norman guy of her own free will—" Rick began.

Olivia knew a refusal when she saw it coming. Quickly, she changed strategies. "All right, then go after him for stealing my jewelry. I'll press charges. Whatever it takes to get him out of my sister's life and mine, I'll do it."

"I'd be careful how I phrase that if I were you," Rick warned her.

Olivia felt her back going up. She'd been through a lot these past few days and there was precious little left to her patience. "I'm a lawyer, I don't get careless with words, Sheriff."

"And there's abandonment," Lupe chimed in, speaking up for the first time. "You could get this guy for that."

The word "abandonment" suddenly sank in. Olivia realized that with her mind racing a hundred miles an hour and going off in all different directions at once, she'd gotten so caught up in finding the baby, she hadn't asked the sheriff a very basic question. There was a huge chunk of information she was missing.

"What are you doing with my nephew in the first place, Sheriff? Why do you even have him?"

"I found your nephew on my doorstep this morning when I was leaving for work," he informed her matter-of-factly.

"On your doorstep?" Olivia echoed, stunned. "That's impossible. Tina would have *never* let Bobby out of her sight." She paled as a possible explanation came to her. "Unless something's happened to her." Her eyes widened as she caught hold of the sheriff's arm, a sense of urgency telegraphing itself from her to him. "Sheriff, you've got to help me find—"

"Don't go getting ahead of yourself," Rick told her. He thought of one plausible explanation, although it was a stretch. "Maybe your sister figured that what was ahead was too dangerous for the little guy."

He was being kind, making up an excuse to calm the blonde with the ice-blue eyes. In his heart, though, he believed that perhaps the woman's sister had gotten bored with playing house and had decided to abandon her latest toy, leaving him in the first place that came up. Maybe they'd passed his place on their way out of town and impulsively decided to drop the baby off on his doorstep.

Technically, his mother had done that, Rick thought, leaving him and his younger sister, Ramona, with her mother-in-law. He could still remember what she'd looked like as she'd promised to be "back soon."

"Soon" had turned into close to eighteen years. By the time she actually *had* returned, he didn't need her, or her lies, in his life. She'd come back too late. He'd grown up with a substitute mother, his tough-as-nails grandmother, molding his life and Mona's. Maria Elena had been a hard taskmaster, but her heart had been in the right place and she had made him the man he was today. And for that, he would always be grateful to the pint-size martinet.

"Or maybe Don felt that the baby was dragging them down and he told my sister to get rid of Bobby—or else," Olivia said.

"But he is the baby's father, isn't he?" Lupe asked, horrified.

"The baby's his," Olivia allowed slowly. "But it takes

more than getting a woman pregnant to make a man a father," she said with feeling, raising her chin.

Rick saw the anger in her eyes and found the sparks oddly fascinating.

"That vermin has no more of an idea on how to be a father than a panther knows how to walk around in high heels," Olivia declared angrily.

"Interesting imagery," Rick commented. He glanced down at her feet and saw that she was wearing fashionable shoes whose heels could have doubled as stilts. They had to be around five inches. How did she manage to walk around in them?

"Feet hurt?" he guessed.

They did, but that was something else she wasn't about to admit. Besides, she'd gotten used to the dull ache.

"No," she denied. "Why do you ask?"

"Haven't seen heels that high since the circus came through a couple of years ago." He glanced at her shoes again, shaking his head. The women he knew were given to jeans and boots. But on the other hand, he had to admit the woman had a great set of legs. Best he'd seen in a very long time. "They just look like they might hurt."

She lifted the shoulder the baby wasn't leaning against in a partial shrug. Bobby'd fallen asleep and she wasn't about to disturb him. Olivia lowered her voice. "That all depends on what you get used to," she told him, the inflection in her voice distant.

The woman wasn't kidding when she said she knew her way around words. "I suppose you have a point. By the way," he said, and extended his hand toward her. "I'm Sheriff Enrique Santiago—Rick for short."

There was no way this man came up short in any category, Olivia caught herself thinking before she blocked any more personal observations.

Where was her mind?

Impatient with her oversight—names should have been exchanged immediately—rather than put her hand into his, she wrapped her fingers around his hand, automatically assuming the dominant position. "Olivia Blayne."

"Olivia?" he echoed. She couldn't tell if the sheriff was amused or charmed. "Now there's a name you don't hear every day." Amused, she decided, he definitely sounded amused. Why? "What do they call you?" he asked.

Undoubtedly he was waiting for her to render up a nickname, something along the lines of "Livy," or maybe "Livia." He couldn't possibly be thinking of "Olive," she thought in horror. That name conjured up the image of a certain tall, skinny cartoon character from her childhood days.

There'd been a boy in the neighborhood, an older boy—nine to her seven—Sloan something-or-other, who'd teased her mercilessly. He'd called her Olive because she had been that skinny back then. The nickname had turned into the driving force that motivated her to not only put some meat on her bones, but to get fit as well. She'd been relentless about the latter in her teens.

"Olivia," she informed him tersely. Only Tina got to call her something else. Tina called her Livy, but right now, Olivia didn't know if she was up to hearing that name.

Many thoughts crowded her head. She was far too worried that something had happened to her sister. She was absolutely certain that Tina would have *never* just left Bobby like that. Not unless she wasn't around to prevent it.

Don't go there!

If it turned out, mercifully, that Tina was all right, she was going to kill her sister with her bare hands for putting her through this, Olivia thought angrily.

She took a deep breath, forcing the dark thoughts into the background. Instead, she focused on the infant sleeping on her shoulder. Focused on how good, how soothing that felt, to know that he was safe and that he was here, with her. It allowed her to pretend, just for the moment, that everything would be all right. That Tina was all right.

"Where are you from?" Rick asked.

"Dallas," she told him. A look she couldn't read came into his eyes. "We're both from Dallas."

That was over four hundred miles away. She was a long way from home. "How did you happen to track them to Forever?"

"Luck," she replied. Because she could feel his eyes on her, waiting, she elaborated. "Tina called a friend of hers, Rachel. She told Rachel that she thought she'd made a mistake, but it was too late to change things. Rachel knew I was looking for Tina so she kept Tina on as long as she could. I have a…" Olivia hesitated for a moment, looking for the right word, then settled on "friend at the cell phone's service center."

There was no need to say that Warner had also been someone she'd once cared about until things got too serious, spooking her. For now, maybe forever, she was committed to her career and her sister—and Bobby— and that was more than enough.

"He managed to get the location of Tina's last call to Rachel triangulated. I used the coordinates and came here instead of Nuevo Laredo," she said, mentioning another small town in the area. And then an idea occurred to her as she said the name. "Maybe that's where they went," she said hopefully.

"Easy enough to check out," he told her. "You have a picture of your sister?"

Olivia smiled in response. It was a confident smile, the kind that lit up a room, and a man if he happened to be in the path of it, Rick speculated.

Shifting slowly so that she didn't wake the baby, she told Rick, "I can do better than that."

Yes, he thought, *I'm sure you can.*

The next second, he upbraided himself for his lack of focus.

She put her hand into her purse, rifling around, searching for the copy of the picture she'd almost forgotten to bring with her. She'd had to double back to the condo in order to pick it up. Finally locating the object of her search, she pulled it out and held it up for him to see.

"It's a picture of my sister with the slime."

Rick bit the inside of his mouth to keep from laughing. He had a feeling that Olivia Blayne would interpret it as laughing at her and wouldn't appreciate it.

Chapter Three

Rick studied the photograph he'd been handed.

"Not bad looking, as far as slime goes," he commented.

The woman in the photograph looked more like a girl, really, and clearly resembled her older sister. They had the same golden-color hair, like a spring sunrise in the desert. The same bone structure as well, but while on the girl, it appeared almost too delicate, on the woman in the diner, it seemed far more classic and refined. He could see her moving with ease through influential circles in high society.

Indicating the photograph, he looked back at Olivia. "Mind if I hang on to this for a bit? I'd like to send it out with the APB." Realizing that he was guilty of just tossing around initials that she might not be familiar with, he began to explain, "That's an—"

"All points bulletin," she concluded for him. "Yes I know. You don't have to stop to break things down to their lowest level for me, Sheriff. I am familiar with some of the terms used in law enforcement." And then, because she needed something to hang on to, something to reassure her, despite her facade of confidence and bravado, that Tina was all right, she asked, "Did you happen to see my sister when she was in town?"

Rick took another glance at the photograph. Though he sensed she wanted to ask him questions about her sister, about her condition and how she'd seemed to him, he'd seen neither of the two individuals she attempted to locate.

He shook his head. "Sorry, I didn't."

Miss Joan ceased overcleaning the counter and spoke up. "I did."

Olivia instantly gravitated toward the owner of the diner. "How did she look? Was she all right?" Though Olivia had never seen any firsthand evidence of it, she strongly suspected that Don had a temper. Without a hovering older sister, he'd be free to treat Tina any way that he wanted to.

The very thought brought a numbing chill down her spine.

An intuitive look came into Miss Joan's kind hazel eyes. "I didn't see any bruises, if that's what you're asking," the older woman told her. "But your sister did look like she could do with a decent meal and about a day's sleep. I felt sorry for her, but there wasn't anything anyone could do." There was more than a trace of regret in Miss Joan's voice. "The guy she was with kept her on a real short leash. And he didn't seem too happy about this little fella fussing and crying," she added, nodding toward Bobby. "In my opinion, someone needs to take that boy behind the barn for a good whopping."

Rick could see the woman beside him growing progressively tenser. Olivia's hands fisted, even as they held the sleeping baby against her, and her expression hardened.

"Shooting him would be better," Olivia murmured with feeling.

He had a feeling she meant it. The woman certainly wasn't the squeamish type, he thought. The sooner he tracked down the missing pair and sent them all on their way, the better.

Sliding off the stool, he saw the question in her eyes. "I'm going to go post that APB, see if anyone's seen your sister and her boyfriend. You wouldn't happen to know the kind of car they were driving, would you?"

Not only did she know the kind of car they were driving, she rattled off the make, the model, the color and the license plate for him in a single breath, right down to the long scratch on the driver's side bumper.

"You've got a good eye," Rick commented, impressed. In his experience, women who looked like Olivia Blayne didn't know their way around cars, much less absorb that much about them.

"I've got a good memory," she corrected. "Don doesn't have two nickels to rub together. The car belongs to Tina. I bought it for her when she graduated high school."

"Wish I had a sister like you," Lupe said wistfully. A look from Miss Joan had her going back to filling sugar dispensers.

Rick hadn't heard what Lupe said. He was busy studying Olivia, trying to get a handle on her. She sounded more like an indulgent parent than an older sister.

Aware of the sheriff's penetrating scrutiny, Olivia called him on it. "What?"

"Let me get this straight. You bought your sister a car. If I understood correctly what you said, she lives with you and you took in her no-account boyfriend even when you didn't want to." Most women Olivia's age either lived on their own or with a lover, not a younger sister and that sister's deadbeat boyfriend. At least not if they could afford a place of their own, as she so obviously could.

Olivia seemed impatient for him to get to the point. "Yes?"

"Well, looking at those kinds of facts, I'd guess that you were compensating for something." His eyes held hers. She knew she could turn away at any time, but she decided to face him down. "Were you?" he pressed.

Her first impulse was to indignantly say no, but she wouldn't cut this short. She'd always zealously guarded her privacy, hers and Tina's. Her second impulse was to tell this would-be Columbo in boots and a Stetson that it was none of his damn business and just walk away. But she couldn't.

She needed him.

Finding Tina would take a lot longer if she went about it on her own and the man had resources he could tap. Those resources could prove very useful and time saving in the long run.

Besides, she assumed that he was familiar with the area. She definitely wasn't. That all added up in his favor, even if he was too nosy for her own good.

Since the sheriff continued watching her, quietly waiting for a response, she had to tell him something. Otherwise, she ran the risk of alienating the man. And while alienating people normally didn't bother her, this time it might prove to be a liability.

Oh, damn it, Tina, why couldn't you just stay put? Why are you such a flake? What would Mom and Dad say if they were alive now?

If they were alive now, none of this would have happened. Tina had adored their father and would never have done anything to incur his disapproval.

Instead, Tina had become involved with someone who had no redeeming qualities whatsoever, gotten pregnant and then irresponsibly run off. And on top of that, from at least outward appearances, she'd abandoned her baby. Something like that could get her locked up for a long time in a place like this, Olivia thought.

After a moment's debate, she decided to tell the sheriff something she didn't normally share. None of the people at the firm where she worked were aware of this. But maybe if Santiago knew, it would make him go easier on Tina.

Right now, she could see that he wasn't about to nominate her sister for Mother of the Year, or even of the hour. And she just wanted to take Tina and the baby home, not hang around to do battle over any kind of charges he would want to bring against her sister.

Taking a breath and mentally bracing herself for the words she was about to say, Olivia began. "Ten years ago, my parents were gunned down in the jewelry store they operated." The corners of her mouth curved in a humorless smile. "Gunned down for two hundred twenty-three dollars and seventeen cents. That was all the money that was in the register. The rest were credit card receipts that did the thieves no good.

"My sister," Olivia continued grimly, "was in the store at the time, in the back, doing her homework. The gunmen never saw her, but she saw them and what they did. I couldn't get her to talk for a week."

She remembered rushing home from college. Remembered the awful, empty feeling inside her as she'd identified the lifeless bodies of the people who had once filled the corners of her world so richly, so lovingly.

"Tina started acting out shortly after that, getting into fights at school. Crying at the drop of a hat. She was always afraid to go out by herself, always looking over her shoulder." Olivia looked up at him and lifted one shoulder in an almost hapless shrug. "I did what I could to make her feel safe."

Rick didn't follow her reasoning. "By giving her things?" he asked.

Olivia inclined her head. "Among other things," she allowed. She could see the sheriff didn't understand. Most men wouldn't, she supposed. "Possessions give you a feeling of stability, of continuity. Owning something *feels* good."

Rick laughed shortly. The sideways logic interested him, not that he bought into it.

"Then Ed Murphy must feel really stable," he commented. When she raised a quizzical eyebrow in response, he told her, "Ed's one of Forever's more eccentric citizens. He's always pawing through things other people throw out. A lot of that stuff finds its way into Ed's one-bedroom house. I hear it's like a rat's nest in there these days."

She didn't know if he was just relating a quaint story or subtly ridiculing her. Sheriff Enrique Santiago looked like a simple man on the surface—sexy as all hell, but simple—but she had a strong suspicion that beneath those prominent cheekbones was a rather shrewd, logical man.

For now, she decided to reserve her final judgment, at least for a little while. She hadn't gotten to the position of junior partner in her rather highly regarded, high-profile firm so quickly by making hasty decisions and snap judgments.

"About that APB," she prodded.

"On it," he assured her. With that, he turned on his heel and started for the door. When she followed him, shadowing him step for step to the door, he stopped short. "Are you coming with me?"

She smiled. "Can't put anything over on you, can I?" she asked in what she hoped he'd take to be a teasing manner. She had to keep reminding herself not to get on his wrong side and that she needed him.

He glanced at Miss Joan. "I figured you'd be more comfortable staying here." And he would be more comfortable going about his job without having her less than five feet away.

"Comfort isn't my main priority," she informed him, her voice growing more serious. "If you don't mind, I'd like to go with you, see what you do."

Having a beautiful woman around was way down on his list of things he minded. But, in this case, he knew it wasn't just to keep him company. "Don't trust me to send out that APB?"

He *was* sharp, she thought. He seemed a little too laid-back for her taste and she just wanted to make sure that he did everything he could to locate Tina. But she knew that admitting as much would be a tactical mistake, male egos being what they were, so she forced another smile to her lips, one that was a little sensual around the edges, and said, "No, I just like leaving myself open to new experiences."

The amused smile that came to his lips told her that she could have phrased that considerably better.

She was tired, Olivia thought, and there was no denying that emotionally she'd been through the ringer these past forty-eight hours. That was the reason she wasn't at the top of her game.

"Nice to know," he responded.

She could have sworn a twinkle had entered those incredible green eyes.

Or what could have passed for one, she amended silently. Seeing as how she'd never encountered a "twinkle" before that wasn't captured within an old-fashioned string of Christmas lights. Like the ones her father used to string up around the house during the holidays, she remembered fondly.

The next moment, Olivia felt a pang in the center of her chest. That she missed her parents went without saying, but she missed them the most around this time of year. Thanksgiving this year had been spent with her searching for Tina, an emptiness eating away at her as she stopped at one diner after another, encountering dead ends and pitying looks.

She didn't even want to think about what Christmas might be like if she didn't find Tina.

Decorations had started going up all over Dallas right after the pumpkins had been put away. That only prolonged her nostalgia and the sadness that inevitably overtook her. There was a very real chance that this year, she would wind up spending Christmas alone. Alone because she'd lost touch with all her friends in her drive to succeed, to give Tina a sense of stability and try to meet her every need. Alone because Tina wouldn't be there.

Damn it, since when did you turn into this maudlin, self-pitying creature? Your life is what you make it, so make it good, Livy, make it good.

Besides, she wouldn't be alone. If nothing else, Bobby would be there and Bobby needed her.

She hugged the baby to her a little tighter.

"Hey, aren't you forgetting something?" Miss Joan called out after them.

Olivia turned around, reaching into her purse with her free hand. Obviously the woman had changed her mind about being generous. Just as well.

"I offered to pay you," Olivia reminded the woman, crossing back to the counter.

Miss Joan merely shook her head, a patient, tolerant expression on her face.

"I was talking about the baby's infant seat," she said, pointedly holding it up. Olivia had left it on the counter after taking her nephew into her arms.

Rick was at her side in two steps, picking up the seat.

He nodded at Miss Joan. "Thanks." With that, he was back at the front door in time to open it for Olivia and the baby. The latter began to rouse from his all-too-short nap.

"I think he might be hungry," Miss Joan speculated,

raising her voice so that they would hear her as they walked out of the diner.

Stopping again, Rick looked at Olivia. He hadn't thought of that. For the most part, babies were beyond his realm of expertise. "She has a point. I could swing by the grocery store," he volunteered. "Pick up some milk and a baby bottle—"

"Or we could go to the backseat of my car," Olivia interjected, stopping him before he could go any further. "I packed a few bottles and some formula for Bobby before I left. Tina only took one bottle with her." A smile that was equal parts affectionate and long-suffering resignation came over her lips. "Tina doesn't exactly plan things out."

But Olivia wasn't like her sister, Rick observed. She came prepared. He found that to be an attractive quality in a woman.

"She's not alone," he told her. "I see that a lot as sheriff."

Olivia unlocked her car. "You can put the seat in the back," she told him.

Seeing as how the diner was barely five feet away, he found the fact that she'd locked her vehicle before leaving it amusing. People didn't lock their doors in Forever, much less their cars. In part that was because people trusted one another around here. In part it was because there wasn't all that much worth taking. It all worked out in the end.

And all that did was remind him that his job was superfluous. A halfway intelligent monkey could handle it. He needed something more challenging.

No sooner had he deposited the seat into the back

than Rick found himself on the receiving end of Olivia's nephew, who was now fully awake and not in the best of moods.

"Hold him for a second," she said after the fact.

He cradled the infant in the crook of his arm. "You asking me or telling me?"

"Whichever works," she answered glibly, then inclined her head in a semiapology as her tone replayed itself in her head. He undoubtedly thought she was being too bossy. God knew Tina had accused her of that often enough. "I'm sorry. I have a habit of issuing orders. Comes from taking charge so much, I guess. I didn't mean to offend you."

Secure in his manhood and comfortable in his own skin, it would take a great deal more than a petite blonde in expensive high heels and a designer suit to rattle his confidence. Her apology, however, did surprise him. He would have put money on her never actually apologizing for anything she did.

Maybe you *couldn't* always tell a book by its cover. "No offense taken," he answered. "I was just being curious."

Shifting the baby to his other arm, Rick peered over Olivia's shoulder into her vehicle. He was about to ask if she wasn't worried that the formula might have spoiled in the car, but he had his answer before he got to ask the question. She'd brought along a large cooler filled with ice and baby formula. He noticed that she'd also brought along several packages of disposable diapers. They were piled up on one side.

Rick laughed to himself. Olivia Blayne struck him as the kind of person others gravitated to during a natural disaster. She obviously knew how to think on her feet and was prepared for anything.

Except a runaway sister.

But then, if he was being honest with himself, he still wasn't a hundred percent convinced that her sister hadn't opted to run off rather than have every moment of her life planned out by a well-intentioned but highly dictatorial older sister.

Or at least that was what he would have surmised Tina's feelings to be on the matter.

If it wasn't for the fact that the baby had been left on his doorstep, Rick had to admit that he would have been inclined to just let the whole matter go, even if the woman making the charge was, hands down, the most gut-tightening attractive woman he'd laid eyes on in a very long time.

Beauty-contest-winner pretty or not, though, that still didn't make Olivia Blayne right, he thought.

Bottle in hand, Olivia straightened up, hit the lock on the rear door and closed it.

"Do you have a microwave or a stove where I could warm this up?" she asked, indicating the chilled bottle in her hand.

"We have a microwave," he assured her. There was one in the small room where he and the others took their lunch and occasionally, when he had someone sleeping it off in their only cell, their dinner. "We got it just after we learned how to make fire by rubbing two sticks together," he couldn't resist adding.

Olivia opened her mouth to respond, then shut it again. She would have to be more careful how she phrased things around this small-town sheriff, she chided herself. There was obviously a vein of sensitivity beneath the rock-solid pectorals.

Taking her nephew back from his arms, she flushed slightly. "I'm sorry, I didn't mean to sound as if I thought you were backward in Forever."

"But you do, don't you?" he asked knowingly. There was no indication that he took offense at that, or even that he found it irritating. "Think it," he added when she looked at him quizzically.

"No," Olivia denied with feeling, then, as he continued to look at her knowingly, she relented. "Well, maybe just a little. This *is* a small town," she said by way of what she hoped he'd accept as an explanation.

"Little or not, progress finds us all," he assured her, then confided in a conspiratorial whisper, "We've even got one of them there newfangled com-pew-ters. Now if we could only figure out how to make it work."

"All right, all right," she surrendered, "point taken. I'm sorry. I'm really not trying to be condescending. Having to track down my sister and Bobby has thrown me off track. I'm usually a lot better than this."

"Looking forward to seeing that," he told her with a wide smile that somehow found its way into her belly a moment before it unfurled.

The next moment, she quickly blocked the feeling that flowed out through her. Olivia deliberately shifted her eyes away from him and wound up looking at the single-story building that housed Forever's police department.

The only thing that mattered, she told herself as she

followed the sheriff inside, was finding Tina and taking her home.

She didn't have time to think about anything else.

At least, not now.

Chapter Four

Humming a bastardized version of "Here Comes Santa Claus," Alma emerged from the back storage closet carrying a huge, somewhat worn cardboard box that looked to be almost half as big as she was. Written across the side in big, block letters, were the words *Christmas decorations*. With a dramatic sigh, the female deputy set the box down on the small table against the wall that functioned as the catchall for everything that didn't have an assigned place within the office. During the holidays, it housed the pint-size Christmas tree as well as any baked goods that generous citizens—or Alma—wanted to send the sheriff's department's way.

Only when she set her burden down did Alma see the sheriff and the person and a half who were with him in the office.

Olivia felt a definite chill as the woman regarded her.

"I see you found the baby's mother." The expression on the deputy's face was far from friendly. It wasn't hard to see what she thought of a woman who left her baby on someone's doorstep.

"No, this is his aunt, Olivia Blayne," Rick told Alma.

Alma's expression softened a degree. "She's been looking for the baby. And for her sister."

"Her sister, the mother?" Alma asked, still eyeing Olivia.

"Got it on the second try," Rick congratulated the woman drily. He glanced at the teeming box the deputy had set down. Once Alma got caught up decorating, there was no stopping her. "Look, I need you to stop decorating the office for a minute and put out an APB for me."

"Haven't started decorating yet," Alma informed him. Resigned that the decorating would have to wait, she held her hand out. "Give me the information." Rick gave her both the paper he'd written on and the photograph of the missing duo. Alma glanced at the photograph first, then looked at the description of the car. Raising her eyes to her boss, she shook her head. "You should've been a doctor, Sheriff. Medical people appreciate handwriting that looks like a chicken did a war dance after stumbling over a bottle of ink."

Joe glanced up from the book he was studying. He'd been taking classes online, intent on eventually getting a degree in criminology. His face remained expressionless as he told her, "You can't say that," in his low, rumbling voice.

They'd been together so long, they were like siblings, she, Joe and Larry, with a sibling's penchant for squabbling.

"Say what?" Alma asked.

"'War dance,'" Joe told her.

Alma pressed her lips together, annoyed. "Why not? You say things like that all the time."

Joe went back to reading. "I'm a full-blood Apache, I can make any reference to Indians I want to. One of the few pleasures that your government forgot to take away from us," he deadpanned.

Alma's eyes shifted toward the sheriff.

Rick raised his hand before she could speak, waving away anything that might have risen to her lips. Friendly squabble or not, he was not about to get pulled into this.

"Just get that APB out for me," he told Alma. "Now."

She sat down at her desk and looked at the paper again. Her brow furrowed as she turned the paper upside down, pretending to try to make sense of what was on the page. But she really couldn't decipher what Rick had written down.

"What kind of a car are we talking about?" she finally asked.

"It's a red Mustang, 2004," Olivia filled in, moving over toward the woman's desk.

"Red Mustang, huh? Shouldn't be too hard to spot," she commented. She moved the keyboard closer and began to type. "How long have they been gone?" she asked conversationally.

"They took off several days ago. This is the closest I've gotten to finding them." Despite the fact that she was swaying slightly in an attempt to soothe her nephew, Bobby was becoming more audible about his displeasure. Olivia turned toward the sheriff and held up the bottle she had in her other hand. "You said there was a microwave around here?"

About to point her in the direction of the back room, Rick decided he might as well take her there himself.

Alma, who was far better at the computer than he, was taking care of putting out the APB. So right now, nothing was on tap except some annoying paperwork that required his attention. The paperwork wasn't going anywhere.

"This way," Rick said, walking in front of the woman and her fussing nephew.

The room that did double duty as a kitchen/break area and storage facility was only slightly larger than a walk-in closet. The window on the opposite wall gave it the illusion of being larger than it was.

Rick pointed out the microwave. It sat in the middle of a table that looked only a fraction more sturdy than a folding card table. The microwave itself had seen better days. It had come to them, a second-hand donation from Miss Joan, who had upgraded the one in her diner.

Olivia shifted the baby to her other side, trying to prop him up on her hip. The boy was still too small for that and she didn't want to have to juggle him while testing the milk. Putting the bottle inside the microwave, she selected a time, then pressed Start. When the oven dinged, she turned to the sheriff and held the baby out to him.

"Hold him, please," she requested,

Now what? Rick eyed her uncertainly. Why was she giving him the boy? "You want me to feed him?"

She opened the microwave and took the bottle out again. "No, I need to test the milk to make sure that it's not too hot for Bobby."

Olivia shook out a few drops on her wrist. Then, because she didn't want to just let the milk slide down her skin onto the floor, she quickly licked the drops up.

Why he found that simple act so sensual and arousing was something Rick told himself he'd have to explore at a later time. Right now, he figured it was best not to go there.

"What's the verdict?" he asked.

She smiled, setting the bottle down on the table for a moment and holding out her arms. "It's warm, but not too hot."

"Like the fairy tale," Rick commented, handing the baby back to her.

"Fairy tale?" Olivia asked, curious. Sitting down, she tucked Bobby against her and started feeding him. The moment she placed the nipple near his lips, he started sucking greedily.

"Goldilocks and the Three Bears," Rick told her, resting a hip against the table as he watched the baby eat. "You know," he elaborated, "too hot, too cold, just right."

"Oh, right." Her mind hadn't gone in that direction for a reason, which she explained. "I didn't take you for the type to know fairy tales."

Rick laughed shortly. "I didn't just appear one day, wearing a badge and a gun belt. I was a kid once, just like you were."

The smile that came to her lips was sad, distant, as if she was trying to access something and wasn't quite successful. She looked down at her nephew, taking comfort in just watching him. "I don't remember ever being a kid. It feels like I was always an adult."

He read between the lines, remembering what Olivia had said to him earlier. "How long have you been at it?"

Her eyes met his. "'It'?"

He nodded. "Taking care of your sister."

She didn't even have to stop to think. She could have told him the figure in months if he'd wanted it that way. "Ten and a half years."

No wonder she didn't remember having a childhood. She practically hadn't. She had to have been in her teens when she'd taken on the responsibility. "That's a long stretch."

She smiled at his choice of words. "You make it sound like a prison sentence."

He paused for a moment, his eyes on hers. The woman didn't sound bitter about it, which he found impressive. "Is it?"

"No," Olivia said with feeling. "I love my sister." She didn't want him thinking she was being a martyr about this. Nothing could be further from the truth. "Do I wish that Tina was a little more responsible? Yes, of course I do, but that doesn't mean I don't love her."

"Didn't say you didn't." Finished with his bottle, the baby's mouth had traces of formula all over it. Rick took out his handkerchief and gently wiped away the milky substance. "But life's a complicated thing. You can love someone and still find that there are times you don't like them very much."

To be honest, he expected more denials. He was surprised to see that he'd evoked a smile from the woman instead.

Her eyes crinkled a little as she said, "You have siblings." It wasn't a question.

Rick began to tuck the handkerchief back into his pocket and was surprised when Olivia put out her hand for it. He surrendered it to her and watched as she spread it over her left shoulder.

"One," he told her. "A younger sister."

"We have that in common then." Placing Bobby against her shoulder, Olivia gently began to pat the baby's back, waiting for the obligatory burp. "Except that your sister is probably one of those superresponsible types."

He had no idea how she had guessed that. "She is." Then he explained, "Abuela wouldn't have allowed her to be anything else."

"Abuela," Olivia repeated slowly, searching for a match in her memory banks. And then she brightened just as Bobby burped. She kept him there a little longer, in case more was going to come up. She didn't want to risk her suit getting more stained than it already was. Her dry cleaner would probably tear out what little hair he had left when he saw what she wanted him to clean this time.

"That's 'grandmother' in Spanish," she said, pleased that she remembered.

He had no idea why it would matter to him one way or another that she spoke Spanish. After all, it wasn't exactly that unusual. For more than half the population of the state, Spanish was either a first or second language. But it did.

"That it is."

Olivia gleaned a few things from his tone, putting her own interpretation to it. "Your grandmother raised you, didn't she?"

He was ordinarily the one asking the questions, not

answering them, but he indulged her. For now. "She did."

If his grandmother had raised him, that meant that his parents hadn't been around to do it. Did she have more in common with him than she thought?

"Did your parents pass away, too?" she asked quietly, as if the occurrence demanded reverence.

For a moment Rick thought of ignoring the question, or acting as if he hadn't heard her. But she'd probably only ask again. Besides, he wasn't ashamed of his background and everyone around town knew his history anyway. That was both the good thing and the bad thing about living in a town the size of a small, above-ground pool. Everyone knew everyone else's business.

That being the case, there didn't seem to be much point to being secretive. Even if this woman was just passing through.

"I haven't the slightest idea," he answered.

Olivia was quiet for a moment, digesting his answer and taking it apart. She was right, she thought. The sheriff *had* looked particularly incensed when he thought her sister had willfully abandoned Bobby. Undoubtedly that was because he'd been abandoned himself.

Though her expression didn't change, she found herself feeling for him. Her parents had had no choice in the matter. What kind of a mother willingly walks out on her child?

Olivia lowered her eyes, cradling Bobby in her arms. "Oh."

For reasons he didn't quite fathom, he wasn't annoyed, he was amused. "That was a really pregnant 'oh.'"

Olivia shrugged, pretending to be engrossed in cleaning away the telltale signs of Bobby's last burp from his little round face. "Sorry. I didn't mean to pry."

The hell she didn't. "You said you were a lawyer, right?"

This time, she did raise her eyes and look at him. "Yes."

"Isn't that inherent in your nature, then? To pry?" He rephrased it to seem less hostile. "To find things out?"

"I'm not being a lawyer right now," she told him, letting down her guard. His sharing something private with her had stirred her compassion. "I'm just a worried aunt and sister." She paused for a moment. "And I'm sorry about your parents."

He eyed her quizzically. "What about my parents?"

Maybe she shouldn't have ventured onto this ground, but for a moment, there had been a connection, a kindred feeling. And, since she had opened this door, she might as well walk through the doorway with dignity.

"About them not being there for you," she told him. "I know what that feels like."

He didn't doubt that she *thought* she knew what that felt like. But their situations were ultimately very different. "How old were you when your parents—"

"Nineteen," Olivia answered quickly.

"Then you don't know," he said matter-of-factly. "I was eleven." The world looked a lot different to an eleven-year-old than it did to someone who was mostly grown. "My sister was six. My father had been long gone by then. One day my mother dropped us off with her mother-in-law, saying she'd be back soon," he recounted, trying his best to separate himself from his words. "Turns out that she and my grandmother had a difference of opinion when it came to the meaning of the word 'soon.' To my grandmother it meant a couple of days at the most." Rick shrugged. "Probably less."

"And to your mother?" She had a feeling she knew the answer.

He set his mouth grimly. His eyes were steely as he said, "Fourteen years."

That was still less time than she'd thought, Olivia said to herself.

"Hey, Sheriff," Alma called from the next room.

Rick straightened, moving away from the table. He was glad for the interruption. He wasn't sure what had come over him, but he'd shared far too much with this woman who'd been a complete stranger to him an hour ago. Shared a hell of a lot more than he normally did with people he actually knew.

He had no idea what had compelled him to run off at the mouth like that, except that there was something about her eyes, something that transcended rules and decorum and seemed to pull the words out of him.

Though it sounded absurd, it was as if the woman was looking right into his soul.

Asking him to look into hers.

He was applying for this job in Dallas just in time. A few more months in Forever and he'd be ready for the loony bin. Maybe sooner. There was absolutely no earthly reason for him to be waxing philosophical like this.

People who sat around spinning theories about why someone did or didn't do something ordinarily annoyed the hell out of him—and here he was, voluntarily joining the ranks.

Definitely time for a change of scenery, a change of venue.

Rick got his mind back on business and away from wondering what other threads he and the woman with the hypnotic blue eyes had in common.

"Coming," he called back to Alma.

Before he could cross to her, Alma told him, "I think I found a match."

Olivia's heart leaped into her throat. She had no idea why a feeling of dread suddenly washed over her. This was what she wanted, to find her sister. Why then was she afraid to hear what the sheriff's female deputy had to say?

Feeling as if she was getting up on borrowed legs, Olivia rose to her feet and followed the sheriff into the main room, every step she took resounding in her head and body.

"That was fast," Rick commented to Alma. He glanced at the monitor beside her computer.

"People remember a red Mustang," Alma said. "Especially one that crashed into a utility pole."

"Crashed?" Olivia cried, struggling to rein in the deep fear that seized her heart.

For a second, she couldn't breathe. That was the anxiety kicking in, she told herself, trying to work her way out of the terror that threatened to overwhelm her.

She wasn't going to pass out, she told herself firmly. She *wasn't*.

All she needed to do was just hang on for a second and the room would stop spinning and settle back into place. Silently, she talked to herself the way she did to a nervous witness when she was taking a deposition. Calmly. Soothingly.

"Yeah," Alma said in response to the single-word question. The deputy shifted her chair so that both Rick and the woman with him could clearly see what was on her monitor. She pointed to the bottom of the monitor, where the short notification started. "It says here that there was an accident." She began to read. "A 2004 red Mustang, heading northwest, was clocked going about ninety-five miles an hour when it suddenly swerved and careened into a utility pole."

Holding Bobby tightly against her, Olivia stared at the screen. She tried to read, but none of the words sank in.

"Does it say if they—if they—"

Olivia couldn't bring herself to say the words that were tantamount to ushering in death. Instead, she went at the information from another angle.

"Does it say if they're all right?"

Standing behind her, Rick had quickly scanned the report himself. It wasn't very long.

Turning toward her, he said, "Looks like you're not going to be having any more trouble with your sister's boyfriend."

She knew what that meant, but she needed to hear him say it. "Don's dead?"

The sheriff nodded. "Says here he died instantly at the scene."

Oh God, oh God, oh God. She couldn't stand the man, but she hadn't wanted to see him dead—just gone.

Her mouth felt utterly dry as she pushed the next words out. "And my sister? Tina? Was she—"

He spared her the agony of finishing the question. "She was badly injured. They took her to Pine Ridge."

She didn't understand. "But it says here that the accident happened in Beaumont."

"It did," he told her. "But Pine Ridge is the site of the closest hospital."

That meant that her sister was alive. They didn't transport dead people to the hospital; they took them to the morgue.

She looked at the sheriff, her heart pounding. "But she's alive, isn't she?" she asked in a whisper. If she raised her voice she knew it would crack.

He nodded, and his voice was gentle as he answered, "According to the feedback."

It was a noncommittal answer, but she'd take it. She desperately needed to hang on to something while she pulled all the threads together—again.

"Okay," Olivia said, trying to center herself, to gather the thoughts that were scattered in all different directions. "Okay," she repeated. "We'll go to Pine Ridge. Bobby and I will," she clarified.

"You'll need directions," he told her.

No, she thought, she'd need strength, but there was no handy dispenser lying around to give her some of that. She had to dig it up and tap into it.

In response to his observation, she shook her head. "No, I don't need directions, I've got a GPS. I'll be all right." *And, please God, let Tina be the same.* "Thanks for all your help," she said as she quickly hurried out of the office.

Chapter Five

Rick wouldn't have been able to say why he followed her outside. Maybe it was a sense of duty mingled with curiosity. He'd already decided that she was a stubborn woman and, for the most part, stubborn people both irritated him and turned him off.

But not her.

And if asked, he wouldn't have been able to explain exactly why.

Maybe that was where the curiosity part came in.

She looked around, as if to decide which direction to take in order to find the diner. It was obvious that she wasn't exactly a tracker.

Amusement pulled at the corners of his mouth. Common sense kept it from surfacing. "At least let me drive you over to the diner," he offered.

She would have wanted to say no, but that would be living up to the old adage about cutting off her nose to spite her face. She wasn't sure which way to go to get to the diner and she didn't want to ask the sheriff because it would make her seem stupid. The people around here were probably born tracking.

"That would be very nice of you," Olivia said. "Thank you."

"No problem." He opened the rear passenger door so she could deposit the infant seat and then the infant.

Ultimately it took almost less time for him to drive back to the diner than it did for Olivia to secure the infant seat in the rear of the police car. She remained in the back with her nephew for the short hop back.

He glanced in the rearview mirror, his eyes meeting hers. "She's going to be all right," he assured her with quiet confidence.

Had there been something in the report he hadn't mentioned? "How do you know that?" she asked.

"I don't," he admitted. She felt her spirits dip drastically. "I just know it helps to keep a positive thought."

"Right," she murmured, looking out the window. All the positive thoughts in the world hadn't kept her sister from running off with that lowlife.

Bringing the vehicle to a stop, he was quick to get out. Rick rounded the hood and was at the rear passenger door, opening it for her before she had a chance to remove the seat belt she'd secured around Bobby's infant seat.

He stuck his head in and nodded toward the baby. "Let me take him for you."

She was about to say that she didn't need his help. The words rose automatically to her lips. But while that might be true in this instance, letting the sheriff take the baby allowed her to exit the vehicle with some semblance of modesty, rather than just sliding out with the baby in her arms and her skirt up somewhere between her thighs and her waist.

Once she was out, rather than hand over the baby to her, Rick walked to her car. There were now several other cars parked in front of the diner, but he had no trouble finding hers. Even if he hadn't seen her retrieving the bottle and formula from the cooler, he would have known the vehicle was hers. They tended toward practical cars around here, mostly four-wheel drive and all-terrain vehicles.

No one in Forever had an expensive car that was just for show. Certainly not a Mercedes.

A sense of practicality didn't keep him from admiring her car, though. It was a beauty.

Like the woman who drove it.

Where the hell had that snuck in from? he wondered, caught off guard. It seemed to him that he was paying a hell of a lot of attention to someone who was, at best, just passing through. It wasn't like him.

Still, he was a servant of the people. Or so it said somewhere in his job description. The term that was used was "people" not "just the citizens of Forever." That meant, in an odd sort of way, he was her "servant" as well.

So he asked the kind of question a concerned servant was wont to ask.

"Are you sure you don't want me to take you to Pine Ridge? It's easy to get lost around these parts. Some of the towns around here never even make it to a map. Just a cluster of a few buildings with a handful of people in them."

Having opened the rear passenger door, Olivia was trying to secure the infant seat to the cushion and having less than complete success. Why was she all thumbs like this?

The sharp pain in her heart told her that she knew the answer to that. Olivia didn't want to go there. She did anyway, albeit involuntarily. She wasn't thinking straight because she was worried about Tina. Worried that, even now, it might be too late. That Tina was dying this very minute.

Olivia banished the notion from her mind. Instead, she addressed the sheriff's offer. Maybe another time, she might have let him drive her. But right now, she wanted to be alone. In case she cried. She didn't want any witnesses.

"Pine Ridge is large enough for a hospital, right?" she asked, tossing the words over her shoulder as, kneeling on the backseat, she continued to struggle with the infant seat.

Rick found that he had to exercise extreme control to keep from staring at what might have been the best well rounded posterior he had seen in a very long time. Forcing himself to blink, he raised his eyes up toward the back of her head.

He was in time to witness part of her hair coming undone as she hit her head against the inside of the roof. Several bobby pins came raining down, as did another section of her hair.

Still on her knees, she stopped what she was doing and turned around in the car to look at him. "Right?" she asked again.

It took him a second to vaguely recall the initial question. Something about Pine Ridge and being big enough for a hospital. "Right."

"Then it should be on the map." She sighed, wiggling back out again. "That seems pretty secure," she said, more to herself than to him.

She'd drive just under the speed limit, she told herself. The infant seat—and its precious cargo—would be fine if she kept a steady pace.

Even so, for good measure she stuck the cooler on the floor just beneath where the infant seat was. That should keep it wedged in, even without the belts.

"If I could have my nephew back," she said, the corners of her mouth curving just a little. The sheriff looked rather comfortable holding Bobby. She caught herself wondering if he was married and how many children he had. Not that it mattered.

Rick surrendered the baby, placing Bobby in her arms.

"Hang in there, sweetie," she said to Bobby.

Turning, she ducked back into the rear seat, this time to secure her nephew into his seat. And once again, Rick found himself captivated, staring at her shapely anatomy and trying very hard not to let his imagination take over. He reminded himself that, after all, he *was* the sheriff. But then again, sheriffs were not plaster saints.

Out of the corner of his eye, he saw Miss Joan at the diner window, looking out on to the parking area. Observing him with a knowing smile.

That old woman needed a hobby, Rick thought. One that didn't involve turning everything she saw into gossip.

As Olivia ducked back out of the rear of the vehicle, he reached into his breast pocket and retrieved a business card. He'd had fifty printed up when he first took the position some four years ago. He still had close to that number left. The phone number to the sheriff's department was a matter of record. Other than numbers taking the place of the initial two call letters, the department's number hadn't changed. People knew it by heart.

But she didn't.

"Here." He held the beige card out to her. "It's the department's number," he explained. "In case you find you need help with getting your sister home."

She dealt better with adversity and challenges than with kindness. Kindness threatened to undo the barriers she'd worked so hard to construct around herself. Threatened to make her vulnerable. He was offering something that went above and beyond the call of duty.

She tried to give the card back. "Thank you," she said stiffly. "But I won't need it."

"Take it anyway," he urged. He surprised her by placing his hand over hers and urging her fingers to close around the card. "You never know."

"But I do," she contradicted. "I know my limits and my capabilities and I'm perfectly capable of finding this particular needle in the haystack." Again she held the card out to him.

But he wouldn't take it back. "Humor me."

She sighed softly and, because he was so close to her, he felt a little of her breath against his cheek.

The reaction was automatic.

His gut tightened in response. Accompanied by an unnerving tingle.

"All right," she murmured. "If it makes you feel better—"

"It does," he assured her. A beat later, an easy smile underscored his words.

Olivia placed the card on the dashboard of her immaculate Mercedes and got in behind the wheel.

"Thanks again," she said, shutting the driver's side door. Placing her key into the ignition, she turned it.

And heard absolutely nothing.

Frowning, she repeated the process.

With the exact same results.

Her frowned deepened. Olivia removed the key and then reinserted it in the ignition, hoping that the third time would be the charm.

It wasn't.

This time, however, there was a small whimper coming from what sounded like the front end of her car. When she tried turning the ignition on for a fourth time, the small whimper suddenly turned into the very grating sound of metal on metal, and from every indication, neither piece of metal was faring very well in this screeching, unexpected confrontation.

The last go-round had set Rick's teeth on edge. It was infinitely worse than nails being dragged along a chalkboard. He squatted down so that he was level with the open window on the driver's side and asked mildly, "Problem?"

Frustrated, Olivia pressed her lips together. The man knew damn well there was a problem. A problem she couldn't fix. All she knew about cars was where to put the gas. She was willing to bet that men around this area were born with a torque wrench in one hand and a can of motor oil in the other.

With effort, she forced herself to sound civil and not stressed out. "It seems that way."

She didn't have time for this. Every moment she wasted here was a moment that—God forbid—she might not have with Tina.

Though she hated resorting to this, Olivia raised her eyes innocently to his and asked in the most helpless female voice she could muster, "Can you fix it?"

The question amused him. He wondered if the big-city attorney just assumed he could lay hands on the hood and bring it back from the dead.

"Depends on what 'it' is," he told her. "Pop the hood."

"All right," she said gamely, then looked around for an icon on the dashboard that would point her in the right direction. There wasn't any. Though it bothered her to admit ignorance, if she sat there any longer, the sheriff would figure it out on his own. "And how do I do that?"

He congratulated himself on not laughing. "Here, let me pop it for you," he offered.

She slid out and he slid in, taking her place. The seat felt pleasingly warm against the back of his legs, the warmth working its way through the fabric of his uniform. He did his best not to dwell on that, or on the woman who had warmed the seat with her own.

Finding the hood release on the lower left side of the dashboard, just below the steering column, Rick pulled the handle up. The hood made a slight rumbling noise as if it were attempting to separate itself from the rest of the car. Satisfied, Rick got out again.

He raised the hood and looked down into the belly

of the car. Doing so yielded no insight for him. There was no telltale smoke rising up, no cracks that he could readily see. A quick check of the dipstick told him that at least her oil was full and running clean. He let the hood drop back into place, then pushed it down so that the latch would catch.

"Well?" Olivia pressed impatiently. "Do you think you can fix it?"

He shook his head. "I'm afraid this is a job for the mechanic."

"All right," she said. Hands resting on her hips, she looked around for a garage with the appropriate sign hanging out front. She didn't see one, but that only meant that this mechanic the sheriff was referring to had to be located in the heart of this postage-stamp-size town. "Where is he?"

"Fishing."

"Fishing?" she echoed incredulously. This was becoming a nightmare.

"That's what I said," he answered easily. Taking out his handkerchief, he swiftly wiped his hands, then tucked the handkerchief back in his pocket.

"And he's the only mechanic around here?" she questioned.

"Only one we've got. He should be back Monday," he assured her.

"Monday?" Olivia rolled her eyes. "What am I supposed to do until Monday?" She had hoped that everything would be resolved by Monday. That Tina and the baby would be back home and she could be where she belonged. At the firm. "How am I supposed to get to Tina if he doesn't come back until Monday?"

He was as laid-back as she was frazzled. "We could go back to my original suggestion," he said in an even, unhurried voice. "I could take you up to Pine Ridge myself."

There was that, she supposed. But she hated being in anyone's debt, no matter what that debt was. If you were in debt, they could call it in at any time, collect at any time. She didn't like what that implied. Constantly waiting for the other shoe to drop wasn't the way she wanted to live her life.

But in this case, she didn't appear to have a choice. Not if she wanted to be there for Tina—and to see with her own eyes that her sister was really all right.

So she nodded, none too happily. "I guess I don't have any choice."

"No," he contradicted, "you have a choice. You could wait here until Mick comes back on Monday."

With her luck, the mechanic would fall off the fishing boat and drown. But she had another idea, a better idea than having the sheriff as her chauffeur. "Is there anywhere around here where I could rent a car?"

He shot down her hopes with a single word. "Nope. No reason to have one of those. Everyone's got their own car around here."

"Whether it's running or not," Olivia muttered under her breath in disgust. She took a breath and tried to put her best face on. "If the offer's still open, I'd like to take you up on it." God, she thought, it almost sounded as if she was begging.

"The offer never closed," he said mildly.

Apparently tired of playing a passive part and watching through the window, Miss Joan opened the door and walked out of the diner. She stood on the first step, a force to be reckoned with.

"You two can leave the baby with me," she called. "This way, you won't have to be stopping every half hour or so to feed him, or change him, or to keep him from crying."

Stunned, Olivia glanced from the owner of the diner to the sheriff. "How did she—"

"Miss Joan reads lips," Rick explained, clearing up the mystery. "Her parents were both deaf and she wanted to be able to relate to them, see what life was like for them with their challenges."

"No law against readin' people's lips," Miss Joan said cheerfully. She crossed to the Mercedes and looked into the back, where the baby was still strapped into his infant seat. "It's not like invadin' their privacy and readin' their mail," she added with a toss of her head, her bright red hair bouncing about.

"Oh, but it is if they're talking in low voices and have a reasonable expectation of privacy," Olivia countered deliberately.

Miss Joan stopped and awarded her with a long, sweeping look. Olivia felt as if she was being x-rayed. "I forgot, you're one of those lawyer types." The older woman definitely didn't seem impressed.

Startled, Olivia looked at the sheriff. He had obviously told her. When had he had the opportunity to talk to the diner owner about what she did for a living? And what else had he said to the old crone?

As if reading her mind, Rick raised his hands, fingers spread, shoulder level, a man surrendering before the shooting started.

"Don't look at me. Miss Joan has this knack of just knowing things." He smiled at the older woman fondly. "There's some talk that she might be a bit clairvoyant." He said it to humor Miss Joan, not because he believed it for a minute.

She would have opted for the woman being a witch, Olivia thought darkly. Or, more likely, someone who eavesdropped a lot. Whatever the explanation, she didn't like the woman presuming things and just taking over. She liked the idea of leaving her nephew with a stranger even less, especially since she'd come so close to losing him. She was having a real problem with the idea of letting him out of her sight.

Miss Joan had already removed all the straps and freed Bobby from his seat. Taking him into her arms, she was cooing something unintelligible to the little boy and Olivia could have sworn he was giggling. That was gas, correct? she thought.

"She's right," Rick was saying. "We can make better time without bringing your nephew along." The way he saw it, the boy would be better off in one place. "And he couldn't be in better hands than Miss Joan's."

How did she really know that? Olivia wondered. She just had the sheriff's word for it. He was a stranger to her. For all she knew, he could be a serial killer. The diner owner could be one as well. Experts were only now discovering that there were a lot more women serial killers than they had initially believed.

Stop it, she silently shouted at herself. *You're making yourself crazy. For once in your life, take something at face value and be done with it. Graciously accept the woman's offer. You'll be back soon enough to pick up the boy. What are they going to do, sell him into a white slavery ring before you get back?*

Olivia set her mouth grimly. She had no choice, really. If she took Bobby along, she knew the sheriff was right. Bobby would slow them down and she had this uneasy feeling—most likely paranoia, but it was there nonetheless—that she really didn't have time to waste. She needed to get to Tina's bedside as soon as possible. And, with any luck, get to the bottom of why her sister had left Bobby on the sheriff's doorstep. There *had* to be a reason, she silently argued. Tina wasn't *that* much of a flake. She absolutely refused to believe that she was.

So, summoning her best courtroom smile, the one she flashed to telegraph confidence to the people sitting in the jury box, Olivia looked at the diner owner and said to the older woman, "Thank you, Miss Joan. I appreciate the help."

Miss Joan chuckled knowingly as she cuddled the baby against her. "You don't right now, but you will. In time."

Olivia had no idea what the woman meant by that, but she had a feeling that she might regret asking for an explanation, especially given the condition of her nerves. So she merely nodded and let the comment pass, chalking it up to something that only another native of Forever would understand.

Chapter Six

As she opened the passenger-side door and started to get into the sheriff's car, Olivia stopped and looked over her shoulder at her own car. The sports car appeared completely out of place beside the other vehicles, like a debutante who had unwittingly wandered into a soup kitchen.

She glared uncertainly at the sheriff. "Um, is it all right to just leave my car in front of the diner like that?"

The sheriff smiled and Olivia instantly felt her back going up. Was he laughing at her, or at the question? Either way, she felt foolish.

"If you're asking me if anyone's going to strip your car for all those pretty little parts it has, no, they're not. We tend to respect property around here. Besides, Miss Joan's got a dog, Bruiser. Big dog," he added. "Just the thought of Miss Joan letting him loose keeps those with a little larceny in their hearts on the straight and narrow. I wouldn't worry if I were you," he assured her.

Rick got in, put his seat belt on and suppressed a sigh. Olivia was still standing outside the passenger side. Had she changed her mind about going?

He leaned over to the right so that his voice would project better. "Something wrong?"

Olivia unconsciously bit her lower lip. Something new to worry about, she thought. She peered into the car and asked, "Is it safe to leave Bobby here with that dog around?"

Hindsight told him that maybe he shouldn't have mentioned Bruiser. The lumbering, part Labrador, part German shepherd and all puppy despite his advancing age, was exceeding gentle around children, as if he instinctively knew that he could accidentally hurt them if he wasn't careful.

"Bruiser's a lovable lamb when it comes to kids," Rick assured her. "Miss Joan has to yell, 'Go get 'em' for Bruiser to go after someone. And even when he 'gets' them, he doesn't hurt them—much," he couldn't resist adding with a grin.

"Then he *has* gone after someone?" Olivia asked uneasily, looking back at the diner.

"So legend has it," he replied patiently. "It was a trucker, passing through. Didn't think he had to pay for his supper. Bruiser made him change his mind. And it was just the one incident. But that was enough to put the fear of God into any would-be thief." That was the point of the whole story. "Your car's safe. And so's your nephew."

Trying to put a lid on her uneasiness, Olivia slowly sank down onto the passenger seat. She didn't bother with the seat belt. Rick waited, leaving the key in the ignition, untouched. After a beat, she realized he was waiting for her to buckle up, which she did. With a nod of approval, he turned on the ignition.

She felt testy and argumentative and annoyed with herself for being that way, but she couldn't help it. "Tell me, if this place is so law-abiding, why does it need a sheriff?"

Rick laughed quietly under his breath. In private, there'd been times he'd asked himself the same question. The short answer was that it made the people in town feel safe to know someone official was looking out for them.

Out loud, he said, "To make sure Miss Irene isn't sleepwalking through the middle of town at midnight, or thereabout, in her nightgown. Or worse, driving while she's asleep. And there's the occasional drunk who needs to be locked up for the night for his own good."

"Is Miss Irene Miss Joan's sister?" she asked. Just how polite were these people? If she lived here, would she automatically become Miss Olivia?

And why the hell was she thinking about that? She'd rather be marooned on a desert island than live in a place like this.

"The term's a sign of respect for ladies who've seen close to seventy years or so," Rick answered, turning the vehicle toward the right.

Olivia's lips pulled into a thoughtful frown. For all intents and purposes, it sounded as if she'd fallen, head-first, into an old *Andy Griffith Show* rerun. Places like this didn't really exist, did they? Was Forever really this simple, this uncomplicated, full of kind souls, or was it just a veneer under which was a cauldron of bubbling darkness, of secrets that were eventually going to erupt?

Since she wasn't saying anything, Rick glanced in her

direction and saw the frown. In his opinion, he hadn't said anything that was frown-worthy.

"What?" he asked.

"I was just wondering about what you said. About guiding old women in their nightclothes back to their homes and locking up the occasional drunk for his own good." She looked at him, trying to get a handle on the man beside her. He didn't appear to be particularly sleepy eyed. What was he doing in a place like this? "Is that enough for you?"

She knew that it certainly wouldn't have been enough for her. The description he'd given her sounded downright boring and, if nothing else, he appeared to be a very vital man in the prime of his life. Didn't he want to achieve something? *Make* something of himself?

Her question rang in his head. No, it wasn't enough for him. Which was why, he thought, he'd sent in the application to the Dallas police department. Because he kept thinking there had to be something more.

But the topic was personal as far as he was concerned and she was a stranger, albeit a hell of a sexy one. He didn't share personal feelings with strangers—not without a good reason, at any rate.

"It was," Rick said evasively.

Olivia was quick to pick up on the keyword. "Was," she repeated. She studied his profile. "But it's not anymore?"

He turned down another street. "I thought you said you were a lawyer."

"I am."

Olivia noticed that when he took information in, he

nodded. Like now. "Do the lawyers from where you come from dabble in psychology as well?"

She responded to the question with a laugh and a careless shrug. "Sheriff, we *all* dabble in psychology, whether we realize it or not. You do," she pointed out, turning the tables on him.

"Me?" he asked a tad too innocently.

The sheriff's tone told her all she needed to know. That not only was he aware of using psychology, but that he thought he already had her pegged.

Not by a long shot, Sheriff.

Most men she ran into these days thought they had her pegged. In her company only for a few minutes and they began to assume she was ambitious to the point of being driven. They didn't realize that ambition had nothing to do with it. She was carving out a place for herself at the firm for one reason and one reason only.

Security.

She'd had to take care of herself and Tina for all these years. And now there was another little mouth to feed— and to send off to college someday. That took more and more money—money that, it had sadly been proved over and over again, didn't grow on trees. Money that was only generated—if she was lucky—by the sweat of a hardworking brow.

Her brow.

If everything went well and there were no upsets, perhaps Tina would add a little something to the bank account in time, but right now, the real responsibility for taking care of everyone fell on her shoulders and would continue to in the foreseeable future.

So she worked her proverbial tail off and sacrificed.

Predominantly what she sacrificed was her social life. Other than attending office functions, she had no social life to speak of.

In the beginning, when she'd begun to work at the firm of Norvil and Tyler, the friends she'd once had made attempts to include her in their gatherings. But she always had to beg off for one reason or another, because she was working twice as hard as anyone else at the law firm. She was trying to become indispensable.

After a while, her friends stopped asking her to go out with them. By now they'd gone on to live their lives without her.

All she had in her life was her work and Tina. It was enough, she told herself.

"You," she assured him, answering his question. "I'm sure you size up everyone who happens to pass through your town."

"Only if they require my services," the sheriff told her.

There was just a touch of humor about his mouth, enough for her to momentarily wonder just what those services he was referring to were.

Oh, damn, Liv, you are *overwrought, aren't you? Stop having R-rated thoughts about Rick Santiago and focus on what's important. Getting to Tina. Bringing her and Bobby home. Who* cares *what kind of "services" the cowboy with a badge renders?*

She was roused abruptly out of her wandering thoughts when she realized that they weren't leaving town. They were going back to his office.

He pulled his vehicle up in front of the squat building. "Why are we stopping?" Olivia asked. Had he changed his mind about driving her to Pine Ridge after offering to do it? Was this payback for her asking him questions? He didn't seem like the vengeful type, but then, how much did she actually know about this man with the sexy smile? Next to nothing, really.

Rick got out and closed his door. "Just want to tell Alma where I'm going and let her know that she's in charge."

"You're putting a woman in charge?" Maybe the man was more progressive than she thought.

The look the sheriff gave her was patiently tolerant. Olivia could feel herself bristling—and becoming embarrassed at the same time.

"Why not? Alma's good at her job," Rick told her. "Besides, I know I can count on her to give me the biggest bribe." He saw Olivia's eyes darken with disappointment. "That was a joke," he told her drily. "I guess I better not quit my day job any time soon." He paused for a moment and looked into the vehicle. "You might want to make use of the facilities," he suggested, motioning toward the building with his head. "It's going to take us a few hours to get to Pine Ridge."

Olivia pursed her lips, struggling not to take offense. Did he think she was ten? Or the flip side of the coin, did he think she was a doddering old woman who needed to be reminded that she had to go to the bathroom periodically?

"I'm fine, thank you," she said tersely.

Rick shrugged at what he saw as her stubborn refusal. Made no difference to him one way or the other.

"Suit yourself. You don't strike me as the type to

relieve yourself on the roadside, that's all. And the land's pretty flat from here to there. We'll be lucky to see any brush at all, much less find it just when you might have a need—"

"I said I was fine," she repeated, quickly cutting him off before he could get too explicit.

Rick stood where he was for a moment, his eyes sliding over her slowly, as if assessing what she'd just declared.

"Yes, I'd say you are," he agreed. Straightening, he began walking toward his office. "I won't be long."

"I'll wait here," she assured him in case he was going to ask.

"I expect you will," he replied without bothering to turn in her direction.

SHE WISHED THAT THE SHERIFF hadn't made such a big deal about going to the bathroom before they left Forever. She silently blamed him for the fact that she was unusually preoccupied with the thought that she had to go, and that she would *really* have to go before they reached civilization again.

Suppressing a sigh, Olivia stared out the window at the desolation that stretched before them. Granted, as a native Texan, she was more than aware that this was, for the most part, what her home state looked like. But living in Dallas was like living in any large city. A person tended to forget that the world beyond the sophisticated urban boundaries was mostly rural. And when she was jockeying for position on one of the main highways threading through Dallas, desolation like this slipped her mind.

But here it was, miles of nothing with more miles of nothing just beyond that.

Without her trusty GPS or even a map, she had no idea where they were or how far they'd come. Unable to hold back the question any longer, she turned toward the sheriff and raised her voice to be heard above the country and western music playing on the radio. "How much farther?" Olivia asked.

Rick hid his smile and congratulated himself on pulling it off. "To Pine Ridge?" he asked innocently.

Olivia lost her slender hold on her temper. "No, to Disneyland. Of course to Pine Ridge."

The look on his face told her that he thought he saw right through her. "Anyone ever tell you that you've got the personality of a rattlesnake when you're uptight? I told you to use the facilities," he reminded her matter-of-factly.

She made up her mind right there and then that she would rather die before she would own up to needing to use the great outdoors as a not-so-great bathroom. "I'm fine," she insisted. "And for your information, I *don't* have the personality of a rattlesnake. I'm just anxious about Tina."

"Being anxious isn't going to change anything," he told her. Someone on the radio was hawking a contest for tickets to the latest country and western touring concert. Rick turned the radio down. "Might as well just think positive thoughts."

She wondered if the man practiced what he preached. "That's very Zen of you."

One shoulder lifted and fell in a careless shrug. "Don't know about Zen, but I find it helps me cope."

He glanced at her for more than a fleeting second. With nothing up ahead to hit, he could spare the time. "You have bad feelings about something and it doesn't come true, you've wasted a lot of time and energy worrying about something that didn't happen."

"What if it does come true?" she countered. "If you're having all these positive thoughts and they couldn't be further from the truth?"

Her question didn't change his position. "Way I see it, you've got all the time in the world to be upset and mourn over something bad. No need to rush it. And maybe, taking on a happy frame of mind might just help you cope."

Maybe the man never had to deal with anything more tragic than getting jelly doughnut stains off his uniform. He was in no position to give her "helpful" advice. "All this wisdom, maybe you missed your calling. Maybe you should be stuffing fortune cookies."

Rather than take offense, he seemed amused. "Something to think about for my retirement days," he quipped. Rick nodded toward the sign that was coming into view. "You can get yourself more comfortable," he proposed delicately, "over there."

Her eyes widened. "Behind the sign?"

Rick had to bite down on his lower lip to keep from laughing out loud. "No, in the town the sign says we're coming to."

Relieved that they were at journey's end, she looked more closely at what she'd assumed was a billboard ad. Reading it now, Olivia frowned again. What was going on here?

"That sign says we're approaching the town of Beaumont."

"And so we are," he said drily. "Guess that means you pass your eye test."

She was getting really annoyed with his folksy manner. She liked getting results, not the runaround.

"Why are we stopping in Beaumont?" she asked. "You told me that my sister's in the hospital in Pine Ridge. Did they switch her?" she demanded. And if they had, why hadn't he told her before this?

But the sheriff shook his head. "No place to switch her to," he reminded Olivia. "Unless the good people of Beaumont built themselves a hospital in the last few hours."

Olivia dug deep for patience. When she spoke, she said each word slowly and separately, as if she was talking to someone who was mentally challenged. "My question again is why are we stopping in Beaumont?"

Again, rather than be annoyed, he appeared tickled by her bad mood, which only annoyed her further.

"Because, Livy, you need to relieve yourself before you start turning funny colors, and I need to talk to the sheriff to get all the information I can about your sister's accident and also find out the whereabouts of the body."

She was about to snap at him for calling her by the nickname, but the second half of his statement stopped her cold.

"Body?" Olivia echoed as he slowed down and made a right turn down a street. "What body?"

The sheriff's office—a building that made the one back in Forever look as if it was constructed to be state of the art—was in the center of the street. Rick pulled his vehicle up before it.

He looked surprised that she seemed to have forgotten. "The guy your sister was with when the utility pole jumped in front of the car," he replied with just a touch of sarcasm. "Bobby's father," he prompted when she didn't say anything.

Don.

With everything going on, she'd forgotten about Don. Or maybe that was just wishful thinking on her part. In either case, she was relieved all over again that the small-time con artist and would-be musician was never going to be the source of her sister's grief—and thus hers by proxy—again.

She just prayed that there wasn't going to be some other "Don Norman" waiting in the wings to pounce on her vulnerable sister. That Tina would finally come to her senses and select the next man in her life for his personality and better qualities, not the fact that he looked good in a pair of jeans and had seductive, bedroom eyes.

She could only hope, Olivia thought, mentally crossing her fingers.

Kindness and understanding is worth a boatload of sexy, she told herself fiercely.

So why did the sheriff in the little backward town appear to have both going for him? He seemed kind and understanding on the one hand and had sexy, bedroom eyes coupled with one damn fine seat on the other.

Where was she going with this?

A hot shiver ran up her spine.

If she didn't get some rest soon, she would wind up

doing something or at least saying something that would ultimately embarrass her beyond words.

"I'll stay in the car," she told him stubbornly.

She was well aware that this would backfire on her. Maybe, if he stayed in the sheriff's office long enough, she would be able to find a diner or some public place that believed in bathrooms and not outhouses.

Rick got out. "Sun's directly overhead," he pointed out, his index finger indicating where she might glance to find the fiery orb. "You might not want to stay in the car right about now."

He didn't think she had enough sense to come out of the rain, she thought resentfully. Or the hot sun. And it *was* hot despite being the tail end of November. If her car hadn't decided to give up the ghost and play dead, she would have absolutely no reason to be in this predicament. Stupid vehicle was just out of warranty, too. It figured.

Olivia blew out a long, frustrated breath. So far, this had not been one of her better weeks. She just hoped that the worst was behind her and not, God forbid, just ahead.

"I changed my mind," she informed him, getting out and slamming the car door behind her. "I want to hear what the sheriff has to say as much as you do. More," she underscored, "because you don't have a personal stake in this case, and I do."

"I take a personal interest in every case I get," he said evenly, contradicting her assumption as he walked up to the building's front door. He held it open for her and gestured. "After you."

With a quick nod of her head, Olivia walked in front

of him and entered the building. And as she did, Olivia decided that the man was just a tad too laid-back to be real.

She didn't trust the sheriff any further than she could throw him.

Maybe less.

Chapter Seven

If she were to guess, Olivia would have estimated that the small building that housed the Beaumont sheriff's department was somewhere around seventy-five years old, if not more.

The wooden floor creaked in protest beneath their feet as she and Rick walked into the tiny office.

The faint smell of cigarettes mingled with another, mysterious smell that Olivia couldn't readily identify. Maybe that was for the best. Whatever it was, was musty. The office itself was shrouded in semishadow. The midafternoon sun had completely bypassed it, apparently having better places to be. There was a certain chill about the room. And, except for the sound of breathing, it was eerily quiet.

There was only one occupant in the room, presumably the town's sheriff. The heavyset man appeared to be dozing. He had his boots, drastically worn down at the heel, propped up comfortably on his scarred desk. Olivia couldn't help thinking that the man was a portrait of contentment, sleeping the sleep of the just, seemingly without a care in the world.

An amused smile playing on his lips, Rick crouched

down close to the sandy-haired man's ear and loudly cleared his throat.

The older sheriff started abruptly, roused out of a dream he obviously was enjoying a great deal more than the reality he was forced to wake up to.

Rising back to his feet, Rick grinned as he looked down at the other man. "Working hard as usual, I see, Josh."

Swinging his sizable legs down to the floor, Sheriff Joshua Hudson cleared his throat, stalling for time as his brain cleared itself of the cobwebs that had imprisoned it. He appeared only slightly embarrassed to be caught this way. Obviously, it wasn't the first time.

He lifted his chin defensively. "I was just resting my eyes."

"Well, they certainly look well rested," Rick assured him. He stepped back slightly, in order for the man to be able to get a clear view of Olivia, and then made the necessary introduction. "Olivia Blayne, this is Sheriff Joshua Hudson. Josh, this is Olivia Blayne."

The sheriff leaped to his feet, his boots thudding heavily on the wooden floor. After quickly wiping his right hand against his pant leg, Josh extended it to Olivia as he beamed at her.

"Pleased to make your acquaintance," he said, sounding, in her estimation, as if he genuinely meant it.

Her mind on the reason they were here, Olivia had to force a smile to her lips. "Hello."

Rick spoke up for her before Hudson could ask what brought them to Beaumont. "Olivia's here about that car accident that happened on the outskirts of town earlier today."

The sheriff's deep-set, small brown eyes slid over his visitor quickly, making an educated guess as to the exact purpose of her visit.

"You're an insurance investigator?"

"No, she's the sister," Rick said before she had a chance to answer.

She wasn't accustomed to having someone speak for her. The look she shot Rick said as much. From what she could see, the man ignored it.

Olivia noted that Rick's revelation made the heavyset sheriff uncomfortable. Had he a hat in his hands, she had a feeling that he'd be running the brim nervously through his moist fingers. And then she found out why he looked so uneasy.

"Not the boy's sister?" he asked hesitantly in a voice that was far too small for him.

Olivia shook her head. "No, I'm Tina's sister."

"Oh. The girl in the hospital." Hudson didn't look all that relieved over the clarification. It was obvious that he felt badly for her, as well as for Tina. "What can I do for you?" The question was directed at Olivia rather than at Rick. And then, as if his brain was slowly coming around and engaging, he gestured toward the chair next to his desk. "Please, take a seat, Miss Blayne."

"That's all right, I'll stand." Olivia felt far too restless to sit. Coming here, she'd had all she could do just to remain seated in the car. Off and on she had the completely unrealistic urge to leap out and just run to her destination, despite the fact that she had no idea where it was. Blessed with a great many skills, she freely admitted that a sense of direction was not one of them.

The older sheriff bobbed his exceedingly round head

up and down a number of times as he digested her words. The next question he asked momentarily floored Olivia. "Do you want to see the boy's body?"

She never wanted to see Don again, and to view him enshrouded in death was absolutely the last thing she needed. But she knew that Tina would ask after him and her sister would want her to make sure that he was indeed dead.

Olivia knew how Tina thought. Most likely, now that Don was dead, her sister would wind up making some kind of hero out of him, glossing over his shortcomings and focusing on his few semigood points, reminiscing over the one or two actual good moments they'd shared.

If she didn't go to the morgue to see the body, worse, if she didn't verify that Don was really dead, Tina would live out the next few years, if not more, waiting for him to come walking through the door again. She would have bet money on it. Olivia suppressed a sigh. She had no choice in the matter. She had to see him.

Gritting her teeth, she forced the word "yes" out.

Her stomach tightened and she did her best not to succumb to the sick feeling the thought of seeing the man generated. With all her heart—and not for the first time—she sincerely wished that Tina had never gotten involved with Don.

She tried not to dwell on the fact that he could have easily killed Tina in the accident. Hell, maybe that was even what he was trying to do. She wouldn't have put the idea of a suicide pact beyond him. His mind had been twisted enough to savor something like that.

Sheriff Hudson pulled up his sagging khaki trousers,

mumbling something about the weight of the gun belt dragging them down, and gestured for Rick and Olivia to follow him out of the office.

"Doc Moore's got 'im on ice, so to speak." He looked over his shoulder at Olivia. "Didn't know what else to do with him. Nobody to claim him until you came along," he told her. "First dead stranger we've had in these parts in a decade or so. 'Fore my time, anyway. I can take you to the car after you see him," he volunteered. "Harry towed it to his shop. Not that it can be fixed," he confided. "But Harry figures maybe some of the parts can be salvaged. Unless you want the car, of course," he qualified. Slanting a glance in her direction.

"No, Harry can have it," she assured Josh, freely giving up any claim to her sister's car. "I just need to check out the glove compartment."

She wanted to make sure she had the registration and insurance information before the car was stripped down. Someone in the family had to be practical, she thought. And the job always fell to her.

"Sure thing," Josh said cheerfully.

"Thank you," she murmured.

Hudson beamed. Turning to his other side, he slanted a look toward Rick, as if to silently call attention to the fact that the woman had just thanked him. They didn't often see a woman as classy as this one.

"Hey, no problem," Josh assured her.

It occurred to Olivia that this man was the last one to have seen her sister. Any details he could volunteer were more than welcomed. She needed something to cling to, to fuel those so-called optimistic thoughts that Santiago kept pushing.

"And my sister?" she asked. "What can you tell me about her?"

"She was bleeding pretty badly," Hudson said. "But she was definitely breathing. I checked. The ambulance from Pine Ridge came right quick enough and the medical guys took her to the hospital there. Doc Moore said she was pretty banged up, but he thought that she'd make it if they got her to the hospital in time." There was sympathy in Hudson's eyes as he concluded, "Dunno any more than that."

His small eyes shifted from her to Rick and then back again.

"We appreciate the information, Josh," Rick told the older man when Olivia said nothing.

Rick could see that she was having trouble dealing with all this and wordlessly placed his hand to the small of her back, silently communicating his support. In response, he felt her stiffen against his palm, but she didn't pull away.

Rick thought of it as progress.

"I'LL LEAVE YOU alone with him," Dr. Evan Moore volunteered after introductions and explanations had been made.

Olivia raised her eyes to the friendly physician. She appreciated his thoughtful gesture, but there was no need for it. She shook her head.

"No need, Doctor. I've seen all I need to see." And what she needed to see was that the man who had all but literally destroyed her sister's life was truly dead. He couldn't hurt Tina—or Bobby—anymore. And for that she was truly grateful. "Thank you," she added belatedly. With that, she turned away from the body on the table and walked away.

The doctor's next question stopped her in her tracks. "What do you want me to do with the body?"

Olivia set her mouth grimly. She supposed telling the man to feel free to cut Don's lifeless body up for fish food sounded a little too harsh. But there was absolutely no way she intended to go through the time and expense—not to mention mental distress—of having Don's body transported back to Dallas. She wanted him permanently flushed out of Tina's life—and as far away as possible. She'd figure out what to tell Tina later.

"Bury him," Olivia instructed tersely. Turning around, she placed one of her business cards on a nearby table. "Send the bill to me at this address. I'll mail you a check."

"Maybe you could give the doc a partial payment?" Rick suggested tactfully. "As a sign of good faith. Times are hard," he reminded her.

He was right, but she couldn't help resenting it. She should have thought of that herself. She didn't like having her shortcomings pointed out to her.

Wordlessly, without looking in Rick's direction, she took out her checkbook and wrote a check for five hundred dollars. Tearing it off, she crossed back to the doctor and handed it to him.

"If that's not enough," she told him, "let me know. I'll send you the rest." And then, as if reading the man's mind, she added, "Nothing fancy. He doesn't deserve it."

The doctor nodded knowingly. "Nothing fancy," he echoed. He put the check and his hands deep into the pockets of his lab coat. "Consider it taken care of, Miss Blayne."

Before making their way back to Hudson's office, the older sheriff took them to the town's only garage to see what was left of Tina's car.

The air in Olivia's lungs backed up when she first saw the wreckage. The entire front end was pushed in, looking like a crumpled accordion. Seeing it, she couldn't understand how her sister hadn't met the same fate as Don. Or how either one of them had managed to avoid becoming one with the twisted metal.

"You okay?" Rick asked.

She nodded numbly, not trusting her voice to answer him.

The glove compartment door had been knocked off and she could see some things inside the narrowed space. Olivia took out the papers she needed and tucked them into her purse.

All she wanted now was to leave this behind her and see Tina.

"Can we get going now, please?" she asked Rick.

"Absolutely." There was no reason to stay any longer. He'd already exchanged a few words with Josh and satisfied himself that the other man had relayed all the details of the accident. As they passed Josh's office, Rick said with a grin, "You can get back to that dream you were having, Josh."

"Got a better one in mind now, Santiago," Hudson told him, staring unabashedly at the woman his fellow sheriff had brought with him.

Rick didn't have to guess the subject of the other sheriff's new dream. His grin widened.

The grin remained even as he got back into his car. Olivia was already inside, buckled up and ready to go. When she saw Rick's expression, she couldn't help questioning it.

"What?"

Rick started up the car and pulled out. "Nothing," he said, diminishing its importance. Then, because she continued watching him, he said, "Josh's got something new to dream about."

Olivia sighed. The man talked in riddles, giving her bits and pieces instead of a whole answer. What little patience she had was all but gone. "What?"

"You."

He got a kick out of saying that, even though he had a feeling it wasn't being received in the same spirit. The woman needed to learn how to laugh at herself. How to lighten up a little bit.

"Unlike Forever, Beaumont doesn't get all that many people passing through," he said. "It's usually a while between new faces."

From what she'd seen, the town looked to be the size of a postage stamp. And it was off the beaten path, which was probably why Don had chosen to pass through it on the way to who-knew-where. She had no doubt that the town enjoyed very little variety. One day, most likely, was pretty much like another.

"How do they stand it?" she asked.

Not only did the good people of Beaumont "stand it," they seemed to thrive on it, he observed. "They find ways to entertain themselves. I suspect they'll be talking about your sister and her boyfriend and the accident for some time to come."

Olivia couldn't imagine a life like that. Couldn't imagine submitting to it willingly. She suppressed a shiver that threatened to dart down her spine.

"The boredom would kill me."

Rick laughed. "Everybody's gotta die of something." He spared her a long, appreciative glance. "You look like you'd be pretty hearty to me."

Just how deeply had this man analyzed her? And why? She wanted to ask, to have him explain himself and what he meant by some of the things he'd said. But she told herself not to go there. Knowing would only lead to more dialogue and, just possibly, more insight into the man in the driver's seat. She didn't want more insight; she just wanted to find Tina and get the hell out of Dodge, or, in this case, Forever.

Olivia shifted restlessly. "How much farther is it to Pine Ridge?"

He did a quick calculation, glancing at his odometer. "Ten miles as the crow flies."

That would be a straight line. Almost nothing worked out to be a straight line when it came to traveling. Paths were always comprised of twists and turns. "And if the crow is driving a sheriff's car?"

He grinned. "Depends on whether or not he can reach the gas pedal." He saw that his response aggravated her. The lady had a short fuse. He wondered if she erupted for other reasons as well.

Why was he thinking about that? He hadn't had those kinds of thoughts, or questions, since his fiancée had died a week before their wedding. Why now?

"Same amount," he finally told her. "The land's flat."

"I hadn't noticed," Olivia cracked.

The monotony of the road was enough to put a driver to sleep, she thought. Was that what happened? Had Don fallen asleep behind the wheel and crashed into the utility pole?

She needed answers.

"I doubt if there's very much you don't notice, Olivia," Rick commented without looking in her direction.

As a trial lawyer, she'd learned to question everything, to hold everything suspect. Nothing was ever taken at face value, which was both her loss and her strength.

"Trying to flatter me, Sheriff?"

Someone else might have taken offense at that, but he didn't. "Calling it the way I see it, that's all. Besides," he pointed out, "in case it hasn't occurred to you, there's nothing to be gained by flattering you, Olivia."

Impatience ate away at her. Theirs was the only vehicle on the road. And he was going just under sixty. What was the purpose of staying under the speed limit out here?

"Can this thing go any faster?" she asked shortly.

"It can," he replied, continuing to drive at the same speed.

You would think the man could take a hint, she thought, her frustration growing. "In this lifetime?" she prodded.

He glanced in her direction. "Are you asking me to speed?"

Was everything black and white for this man? She hadn't thought that men like Rick Santiago still existed. Law-abiding to a damn fault.

"I'm asking you to get to the hospital before I start collecting social security checks."

"Don't worry, your sister's stable."

She frowned. "More positive thinking?" Olivia asked sarcastically.

He made no comment about her tone, simply said what he felt she needed to know. "Just before we left for Beaumont, when I went into the office, I had Alma call Pine Ridge Memorial and ask about your sister."

"Why didn't you say something?" she demanded.

She had that edge to her voice again, he noted. "I thought I just did."

"I mean sooner," she stressed.

He lifted the shoulder closer to her in a half shrug. "If I did, you might've thought I was making it up just to get you to calm down."

She supposed that he had a point, but if she followed that line of reasoning, why had he picked now to tell her? "And now?"

"Now we're pretty much almost there. It'll help you hang on for the last leg of the trip." He paused, debating. But she would find out this part, too. She might as well be prepared for it. "There is one thing, though."

Olivia braced herself. "What?"

"According to the hospital, your sister hasn't regained consciousness yet."

"She's in a coma?" Olivia cried incredulously. All she could think of was that some people *never* woke up from a coma. "Why didn't you at least tell me that sooner?" she demanded.

"Because it would upset you—just like it's doing

now," he said. "And I figured you had enough to deal with."

She began getting a claustrophobic feeling. "So you decided to appoint yourself my guardian?" she demanded.

He sounded as low-key as she was uptight. "Just trying to help," he told her mildly.

"I don't need any help," Olivia snapped.

He shrugged, letting her declaration slide. "Whatever you say."

She took a deep breath, struggling for control. Struggling to keep from feeling overwhelmed. God, but she wished there was someone to turn to. But there hadn't been anyone there for her for more than ten years now.

She should be used to this by now, used to soldiering on alone. And, for the most part, she was. But that didn't make times like this any easier. And it didn't keep her from longing, every once in a while, for a handy pair of shoulders to lean on....

And what's the sheriff? Chopped liver? He just tried to help and instead of thanking him, you bit his head off and handed it to him.

Taking another deep breath, she let it out slowly, then glanced in the sheriff's direction. She turned her face forward before she spoke. "I'm sorry, I do appreciate everything you're doing, Sheriff. I didn't mean to lose my temper."

Yeah, you did, he thought, but he left that unsaid. "Apology accepted," he told her. "By the way, that's Pine Ridge just up ahead."

A sense of excitement and foreboding mingled inside

her as Olivia sat up straighter, straining to get her first glimpse of Pine Ridge. With any luck, maybe her sister had come out of the coma and she could take her back home.

Startled, she realized that Santiago's optimism was infectious after all.

Chapter Eight

For a relatively small town—Olivia judged that it was perhaps a shade or two larger than Forever—Pine Ridge's hospital was surprisingly modern in appearance. The inside of the building looked fresh and crisp, as if it had been recently renovated. Two storied, it boasted of "over eighty beds," six of which were dedicated to the intensive care unit.

The ICU was where the attending physician, a general surgeon named Dr. Owen Baker, had placed her sister after he and another surgeon had finished operating on Tina for close to five hours.

Feeling increasingly agitated and stressed, Olivia forced herself to let Rick take over. He was the one who approached the woman at the admissions registration desk to ask about her sister. She knew that had she been more clearheaded, she would have resented his acting on her behalf. But now a part of her was grateful to him.

Dr. Baker had to be paged more than once before he finally came to the ICU area to speak to them. Or rather, to her, Olivia silently amended since she sincerely doubted that Santiago was even mildly interested in her sister's condition, despite his disclaimer about taking a personal interest in the people he found himself dealing with.

Narrating a quick synopsis for them—the six-foot-four, prematurely gray surgeon was obviously anxious to be on his way—Dr. Baker concluded by saying, "And now we just have to wait and see. It's out of our hands. We've done everything humanly possible for your sister."

She wanted to ask if he was referring specifically to himself and the other surgeon, or lumping together the staff as well. And was he thus stepping away from the situation, leaving it "in God's hands," the catchall phrase she felt people used to absolve themselves of any guilt.

Personally, she had decided at her parents' funeral that God had better things to do than to dabble in her life. Whatever happened to her—and to Tina—was on her, and she was the one responsible for their lives.

And how's that working out for you?

She wanted to ask Baker more questions, to ask him how well he and the other surgeon fared in their surgeries. Were they usually successful? But questions like that often sounded bitter and, at the very least, antagonistic. It would have sounded as if she was taking out her helpless frustration on the surgeon when the man had probably done his best.

She wanted to get back to familiar ground, take Tina home.

"I'd like to take my sister back to Dallas. Can she be moved?" Olivia asked, fully expecting the man to say yes.

Maybe it came off sounding condescending, but there

were top surgeons in Dallas. No doubt any one of them was better equipped to help Tina than a doctor in this one-and-a-half-horse town.

To her surprise, Dr. Baker shook his head and said firmly, "Absolutely not—unless your goal is to kill your sister. She's definitely not strong enough to be moved. There were serious internal injuries. She has several cracked ribs, we barely saved her right lung, her liver was badly bruised and we had to remove her spleen—among other things."

She could feel Rick watching her. He probably thought she was crazy, too. It didn't matter. She just wanted what was best for Tina, what would give her sister the best chance at recovery.

"Even by helicopter?" Olivia pressed, determined to get Tina the best of care, not have her sister languish here.

A half smile curved the surgeon's thin lips. "Not even by a transporter beam."

Great, the man's a science fiction aficionado. Just the quality she was looking for in a physician. "When *can* I move her?" she asked, not bothering to bite back her impatience.

"When she gets stronger," Baker answered simply, then glanced at his watch.

She knew that was for her benefit, but she still had questions. "And when do you think that'll be?"

"A few days, a week, a month—"

"A month?" Olivia echoed incredulously, staring at the man.

Dr. Baker seemed unmoved by her distress. "Everyone gets well at their own pace." His pager went off and he looked relieved to be able to turn his attention away from his patient's pushy sister.

"Sorry, I *really* have to get back to the emergency room. I should have been back there already," Baker said.

Not waiting for her to say anything further, Tina's surgeon turned on his heel and hurried away. He nodded at Rick before he left.

"He's not sorry at all," Olivia commented to Rick, annoyed, as she watched Dr. Baker disappear around a corner.

Rick's response surprised her. "Can't say I really blame him, the way you were grilling him."

His comment stung. But then, why would she expect loyalty from a man who was little more than a stranger to her?

"I wasn't grilling him," she protested.

Rick laughed shortly. "If you'd grilled him any more, you could've put barbecue sauce on the man and called him done."

Olivia frowned at his interpretation. "Very colorful."

"Accurate," he countered. This wasn't going to turn out well and he had no desire to argue with her. "Why don't we go and see your sister instead of picking fights with the people who are helping her?"

She noticed that he said "helping" rather than "trying to help." More optimism on his part? She found herself wishing she could share in his take on things. It might go a long way in reassuring her. Because, at the moment, all she was feeling was exceedingly nervous. And seriously worried.

"Okay," she agreed.

She did want to see Tina, no matter what condition her sister was in. If nothing else, she wanted Tina to know she was there for her. She'd read somewhere that even when people were in comas they were aware of their surroundings. She could only hope that was true.

"For the record, I wasn't trying to pick a fight," she told Rick. "I just wanted to light a fire under the good doctor, get him moving."

"Looked to me like he'd been moving all day. You're being too hard on the man." The sheriff looked at her significantly. "Not everyone is a streak of lightning across the sky."

Was that how he saw her? Like a streak of lightning across the sky? She knew if she asked him, it would sound as if she was flirting with him and she didn't want to plant any ideas in Santiago's head. She was definitely *not* interested in flirting with him. Maybe, at another time, in another place—and if he wasn't the sheriff of a hick town—

She silently laughed at herself. Basically, she was saying that it would never happen. She was just burying it in conditions. Just as well. She did better alone.

The line echoed in her head as they went to find Tina.

IT WASN'T DIFFICULT locating ICU. Once there, they found that Tina was the only one in the small, isolated area.

Obviously a slow day for traumas, Olivia thought sarcastically.

She was using sarcasm in a desperate attempt to

shield her exposed feelings, even within the confines of her own mind. If she didn't, it was just a matter of time—maybe even minutes—before she wound up breaking down. And if that happened, she wasn't sure she could pull herself back together again.

For a moment, Olivia stood where she was, hesitant to approach her sister, to see Tina up close.

Even at this distance, her heart twisted at what she saw.

"She looks so pale," Olivia murmured.

"I'll be right outside if you need me," Rick told her softly. And with that, he stepped out of the room.

Sensitivity. The sheriff was displaying sensitivity. The next thing she'd be finding out that Forever was the town where Santa Claus and his elves took their summer vacations, she thought.

Taking a deep breath, Olivia slowly approached Tina's bed. Every step literally vibrated through her, echoing a warning, or putting her on some sort of notice.

She wanted to run, but she didn't dare.

The sun came into the room, but all she felt was a darkness that threatened to swallow her and Tina up. Whole.

"Tina?" she whispered once she was at her sister's bedside.

There was no reaction from Tina, no noise at all. Just the sounds of the machines that were attached to Tina, keeping track of her vital signs, feeding her and fighting off whatever infections lurked in the wings, waiting for a chance to envelope her weakened body.

"Tina, it's me, Livy," Olivia whispered. "I came as soon as I could. This was one hell of a hide-and-seek game you played this time." That had been Tina's favorite game as a child. God, but she wished they could go back to that time. "You definitely weren't easy to track down," she told the still figure. "Not like when you were little. But then, you always wanted to be found back then." Olivia took a breath, her voice quavering. "I got the feeling that you didn't this time."

Olivia could feel the tears in her throat, threatening to choke her. She took Tina's hand in hers, wrapping her fingers tightly around it.

Willing her sister awake. Willing her to be well.

Tina's eyes remained closed.

"I found Bobby." She went on talking as if Tina had responded to her. Praying that she would, that her words would penetrate this thick curtain that separated them and bring her sister back to her. "He's okay." She pressed her lips together as she looked down at her little sister. "Why did you leave him like that, Tina, on a stranger's doorstep? Did you know this was going to happen? Was Don threatening to kill you both for some twisted, screwed-up reason?"

The question echoed around the small area, mocking her.

"Oh Tina, wake up, please wake up," she begged, squeezing her sister's hand a little harder. "Talk to me. Tell me what happened. Tell me how to make it all better for you. Give me a clue. I'll take care of you," she promised, her voice cracking, "but you have to give me a clue what you need. I can't keep doing this all by myself."

Olivia gazed down at her sister. There was no indication that any of her words had penetrated, or that Tina was any closer to coming around than she had been a few minutes ago.

No indication that she would *ever* come around.

Overwhelmed and close to the breaking point, Olivia began to softly cry. Once she allowed herself to stray from the rigid path she'd set down, she couldn't quite manage to find her way back.

The tears, the sobs, just kept coming, threatening never to stop.

Olivia felt as overwhelmed now as she had when the police had come to the dorm that bleak, horrible evening to notify her that her parents had been murdered.

The floor beneath her feet had been slowly disintegrating since she'd walked into the ICU and she now found herself free-falling through space with no signs of being able to stop.

Her heart was breaking.

While plummeting down into this blindingly dark abyss, she became vaguely aware of a pair of strong hands gently taking hold of her. Turning her around. And then she was enfolded in warm, comforting arms.

Instinctively, Olivia buried her face against her comforter's chest. She shook as she cried herself out.

She lost track of time.

A minute, an hour, a day, Olivia had no idea how long she stood there, allowing herself to be held, sobbing out her pain.

Gradually, she became aware of a scent. It wasn't the scent of cologne or aftershave or even shampoo. The scent teased her memory, making her think of shaving cream. Familiar shaving cream.

And then she knew who had wordlessly offered his

support, held her while she temporarily ceased being "the responsible one" and just gave in to the hurt, the pain, to the frustration and the sorrow swirling inside her.

The man whose chest became more and more soggy from her tears was Rick.

Olivia struggled against the very strong desire to sink further into the abyss. Taking a deep breath, she raised her head. Her eyes met his.

"I must look terrible," she mumbled.

Rick fished out a handkerchief from his pocket and offered it to her. She was surprised to see that it was neatly folded in four rather than just crumpled and bearing signs of being shoved haphazardly in his back pocket.

"You look like someone who's been through a lot," he contradicted. There was an understanding, encouraging smile on his lips. "Nothing wrong with that."

Nobody would accuse the sheriff of being a smooth talker, Olivia thought, but there was no denying that the man knew how to be kind. She searched for something cryptic to say, something flippant to use as a shield, which would effectively draw attention away from her anguish.

Nothing came to her.

All she could do was whisper a faint thank-you, and surrender the handkerchief once she'd wiped away the tears from her cheeks.

He shook his head, closing his hand over hers and gently pushing it back. "Keep it," he told her. "In case you need it again."

Olivia wadded the handkerchief up in her hand,

sternly telling herself she wasn't going to cry anymore. She'd had her momentary breakdown, now it was time to get a grip.

Tears never solved anything.

"I thought you were going to wait outside," she said, her voice still hardly above a whisper. She was afraid that if she raised it, it would crack noticeably. She still had a ways to go before she was back in control of herself and she knew it.

"I thought so, too," he acknowledged, then nodded toward the wall next to Tina's bed. "But the walls are kind of thin here and I heard you talking to your sister." For her benefit, he lowered his voice. "And I heard her not answering you."

A hint of a smile curved the corners of her mouth. "You know that's not possible, right? You can't 'hear' something that isn't being said."

Rick merely smiled indulgently. "We've got a different set of skills out here," he told her. To her surprise, he took her hand, not like a lover but like a friend. He gave it a gentle tug, encouraging her to come with him. "C'mon."

She didn't have the strength to oppose him, didn't even have the strength to ask him where he was taking her. Because if it was to the car, she wasn't ready to leave, not yet. But rather than offer any opposition, she waited to see where he was going.

When Rick brought her over to the elevator, she allowed a sigh of relief to escape. They weren't leaving. The ICU was on the first floor and all they had to do to get to the parking lot was to walk through the front doors.

Get **2** Books **FREE!**

Harlequin® Books,
publisher of women's fiction,
presents

 HARLEQUIN®

GET 2 BOOKS

We'd like to send you two *Harlequin American Romance*® novels absolutely free. Accepting them puts you under no obligation to purchase any more books.

HOW TO GET YOUR 2 FREE BOOKS AND 2 FREE GIFTS

1. Return the reply card today, and we'll send you two *Harlequin American Romance* novels, absolutely free! We'll even pay the postage!

2. Accepting free books places you under no obligation to buy anything, ever. Whatever you decide, the free books and gifts are yours to keep, free!

3. We hope that after receiving your free books you'll want to remain a subscriber, but the choice is yours—to continue or cancel, any time at all!

EXTRA BONUS

You'll also get two free mystery gifts! (worth about $10)

FREE!

Return this card promptly to get
2 FREE BOOKS and 2 FREE GIFTS!

◈ HARLEQUIN®

YES! Please send me 2 FREE *Harlequin American Romance*® novels, and 2 free mystery gifts as well. I understand I am under no obligation to purchase anything, as explained on the back of this insert.

About how many NEW paperback fiction books have you purchased in the past 3 months?

❏ 0-2
E9L7

❏ 3-6
E9MK

❏ 7 or more
E9MV

154/354 HDL

FIRST NAME	LAST NAME

ADDRESS

APT.#	CITY

STATE/PROV.

ZIP/POSTAL CODE

Visit us at:
www.ReaderService.com

◀ DETACH AND MAIL CARD TODAY! ▶

(H-AR-11/10)

The elevator arrived within seconds of his pressing the down button. Ushering her into the elevator car, Rick pushed the button with the glowing B for the basement on it.

With effort, Olivia finally managed to pull herself together enough in order to begin framing a question. She got to utter only the first word.

"Where—"

"Cafeteria," he replied simply, anticipating the rest of her question. "By my reckoning, you haven't had anything to eat in quite some time."

She raised her eyes to his, her brain slowly engaging again. "Neither have you," she pointed out. They hadn't stopped at a single take-out place since they'd left Forever.

"Exactly. I figure we both need to fuel up. The world always looks a little more manageable on a full stomach," he told her.

Olivia didn't quite see it that way. Food was usually grabbed as she made her way to another destination, nibbled on every so often as she toiled over briefs and opening statements. She never sought out food for its own sake, or consumed it for the sheer pleasure of it the way she once had. This was why she'd never bothered to learn how to really cook.

Right now, she could feel her stomach churning in turmoil, tightening to the point that breathing became difficult. She was clearly running on empty, she thought, but she was far too agitated to sit down for a meal.

"I'm not sure I can keep anything down," she confided.

"Well, this is a hospital. I'm sure I can get someone

to scare up an IV for you if you refuse to eat," he told her matter-of-factly. Obviously he intended for her to eat and was prepared to wait her out until she gave in and ate.

She was about to protest his taking charge this way, acting as if she was some wayward, willful child who couldn't fend for herself. As if she'd suddenly been deemed incompetent.

For a moment, her back was up and she was ready to get into it with him.

But a part of her, a more grounded, clear-thinking part, annoyingly reminded her how badly she wanted someone to lean on, to share a little of the burden that she struggled with. And it was clear this sheriff, from that tiny spec-on-the-map town, was doing just that. He was taking charge, relieving her, just for a moment, of the burden she'd voluntarily picked up over ten years ago.

Sighing, Olivia walked in ahead of him as he held the swinging double doors open.

At first glance, the cafeteria dining area appeared to be only a little bigger than the kitchen in her apartment back home. An elderly woman nursing a cup of coffee sat at one of the seven tables. The other tables were empty.

It was obviously between meals, Olivia thought. A glance toward the food service revealed some things to choose from. A few platters planted on beds of ice maintained their positions behind glass partitions.

"Maybe I can try to keep something down," she told him.

"Every success starts out with someone trying," Rick said, handing her a tray.

One look at his face told her that the sheriff actually believed in the simplistic adage.

Because she was still clutching the handkerchief he'd given her, Olivia kept her negative retort to herself. But she felt relieved that she was beginning to return to her old self again.

Chapter Nine

Olivia discovered that she was hungrier than she'd realized. The moment she put a forkful of the beef stew that the sheriff had insisted on paying for into her mouth, she could feel her taste buds cheer. She ate with gusto, something she couldn't remember doing in the recent past.

She was almost finished when she became aware of Rick observing her. His eyes almost seemed to be smiling as he watched her.

Lowering her fork and raising her guard, she met his gaze. "What?"

"Just nice watching you enjoy something," Rick replied.

She thought of how he'd insisted that she eat. He was the one who had put the stew on her tray, guaranteeing that she'd like it. "You just like being right."

"That, too."

He finished the cup of coffee he'd been nursing. The roast beef sandwich he'd ordered had become history quickly. The dispute over payment of the tab was taking longer to die.

She was accustomed to paying for everything or, at

the very least, her own way. For the past ten years, she'd been adamant about not being in anyone's debt in any manner, shape or form. "I still feel I should pay for my meal."

He wasn't about to get roped into another discussion about this. The price of the stew and her soft drink was not going to break him. Besides, when he came right down to it, he kind of liked sitting across from her at the small table.

"That horse has already been ridden and put away," Rick told her. "A person who really feels in control lets other people do a few things once in a while." She put down her fork, finished. Rick nodded his approval. "Now then, you want dessert or are you ready to go?"

"Go?" The way he asked made her feel that he wasn't referring to making their way back to the ICU and Tina.

"Back to Forever."

That was what she was afraid he was saying. She shook her head. "I can't leave Tina." Not when her sister was like this, unconscious and vulnerable.

The woman was overprotective, he thought. Could be why her sister ran off the way she had. But it wasn't his place to say that. Besides, he had the feeling Olivia would only get her back up if he did. "Seems to me that your sister's in good hands. Her son needs you more than she does right now."

Bobby.

Oh God, she'd forgotten all about him. A huge wave of guilt washed over her, drenching her as it momentarily stole her breath away. How could she have forgotten about the baby?

Olivia pressed her lips together, vacillating, trying to sort things out in her head. The fact that the little boy was some sixty plus miles away presented a definite problem in logistics. She knew she couldn't be in two places at once, but where was she most needed? Tina had always been her first priority, but now there was Bobby. Bobby had no one to take care of him except for her. And to complicate matters more, she didn't even have a running car.

"Don't worry about not being able to come back," Rick said, as if he was reading her mind. "I'll bring you here tomorrow."

She'd assumed that this was a one-shot deal. "But aren't you busy?"

An amused smile played on his lips. "As it happens, I'm in between crime waves, so I've got a little downtime." The smile widened as he added, "You might have noticed that."

He was essentially offering to be her chauffeur. The man didn't know her from Adam—or Eve. Why was he being so nice to her? She'd never liked things she didn't understand.

"It's not that I'm not grateful," she began slowly, "it's just that I can't impose on you like this."

"Nobody said anything about imposing," he pointed out. "In Forever, we take care of our own."

"But I'm not from Forever."

He laughed softly. "Your car's parked in front of the diner. That's close enough."

"I'll pay you for your services."

Ordinarily, stubbornness to this degree irritated him,

but he had to admit that this woman did fascinate him. "No need. Besides, I wouldn't know what to charge."

She had a solution for that. Her whole life was built around finding solutions. "I could make a donation to your favorite charity."

He had a better suggestion. "How about you just pass it on when the time comes?"

She eyed him quizzically. "Pass it on?"

He nodded. "The next time you come across someone in need, help them."

Olivia opened her mouth to protest that she wasn't in need, but she realized that would have been a lie. Because she was. Just because she didn't meet the stereotypical definition of a needy person did not negate the fact that she really was a person in need.

For the moment, she underscored, to make herself feel better.

"Okay," Olivia finally agreed, knowing that any further arguing would be futile and it would make her out to be an ungrateful snob to boot. She balked at the image even as she began to wonder if that was the way she came across. And if so, underneath it all, *was* she actually a snob?

The idea bothered her. A great deal.

She *wasn't* a snob, Olivia insisted silently. She didn't think of herself as better than the next person. But if that "next person" happened to be standing in the middle of Forever, Texas, well, she did feel she was more sophisticated, more polished.

Did that ultimately make her a snob?

Maybe she was a snob. She was also very confused and torn.

In the end, she agreed with the good-looking sheriff. Bobby was her responsibility and right now, he needed her more.

THEY WERE BACK ON THE ROAD within fifteen minutes. And Olivia wound up dozing off within thirty. The monotony of the open road, bathed in approaching twilight, lulled her to sleep.

Hearing her soft, even breathing, Rick glanced in Olivia's direction. He smiled to himself when he realized that she had nodded off. Asleep, she couldn't talk, couldn't argue and he had to admit that, for now, he found her more attractive that way. But then, he was attracted to her no matter what the circumstance. She was a damn fine looking woman by anyone's standards.

He'd already noted that she didn't wear a ring. She hadn't mentioned anything about a husband or significant other waiting for her back home. So, as far as he knew, she was unattached. It made him wonder. An intelligent woman who looked the way she did was one hell of a package. Yet as far as he could tell, no one had taken her home to unwrap.

Was that by choice? And if so, why?

Was there something in her background the way there was in his?

He felt his stomach muscles tighten the way they always did whenever he thought of Alycia. Alycia Banderas. He had been one week away from marrying her when a cross-country moving van had flipped over on its side, crushing not just her car but all of his dreams in one awful moment. That kind of event made a man step back and wonder about how fragile life really was.

He was getting philosophical in his old age.

Well, once he got that job on the police force in Dallas, he doubted he'd have time for philosophical conjecture. His friend Sam had confided that he had trouble finding *any* time to himself. The job claimed the man 24/7. From where he sat, Rick couldn't help thinking that he really liked the sound of that.

OLIVIA SLEPT THE ENTIRE trip back.

She had to have been really drained, he thought, his sympathy aroused. Too bad he couldn't let her go on sleeping, but even if he was so inclined, he wouldn't be doing her any favors. Her neck would be killing her tomorrow.

Forever was just up ahead.

Rick decided not to stop at his office and go straight to the diner to pick up the baby. As he drove past the city limits, Olivia stirred beside him. The next moment, she bolted upright, apparently startled that she'd fallen asleep in his car.

Her neck hurt and the corners of her mouth felt moist. Oh God, she hoped she hadn't drooled, she suddenly thought.

Embarrassed, she mumbled, "I must have fallen asleep."

"Must have," he agreed.

She didn't have to look, she could hear the grin in his voice. Had she talked in her sleep? Or worse, snored? Olivia felt uncomfortable as well as really vulnerable.

"Why didn't you wake me?" she asked, an accusing edge to her question.

Rick shrugged. "Didn't see the point. You were tired. I thought you could do with the rest."

"I should take my turn behind the wheel," she told him. "It's only fair."

The amusement reflected in his expression only deepened. She couldn't shake the feeling that he was laughing at her.

"To you or to me?" he asked.

She barely heard the question. As she looked through the windshield, it suddenly dawned on her where they were, in front of a diner.

The diner.

The one she'd left Bobby in. And that was her car on the right. How long had she been asleep?

"We're here?" she questioned.

"We're here," he confirmed, turning off the ignition. He got out, rounding the hood to open the door for her. But as he drew closer to her car, he glanced in its direction.

What he saw stopped him in his tracks.

An uneasiness undulated over her. What was Santiago staring at?

Opening the passenger side door, she struggled to shake off the last layers of sleep. She needed to be on her toes, to be able to think. She needed—

Olivia's mouth dropped open as she saw what the sheriff was looking at.

"Oh my God," she cried, horror stricken. "My car. What happened to my car?" she asked. She'd left the top down and the upholstery on the front passenger side looked as if a wild animal had gotten in and attacked it.

Stunned, she ran her hand along the jagged fabric. "It's all ripped up inside."

"Not all," he qualified. "Just that section," he said, pointing to the damaged area. "But it does look pretty bad."

The door to the diner opened just then and Miss Joan, holding Bobby in her arms, appeared. For a moment, she simply stood there, as if taking the scene in. And then Rick saw a pink hue of embarrassment across the diner owner's face.

Miss Joan raised her chin, ready to own up to her part in what had happened. She faced it the same way she faced any and all events in her life, good or bad: head-on, showing no fear.

"I'll pay for it," she told Olivia.

Fully awake now, Olivia turned in the older woman's direction. Stunned, shaken up, she didn't know whether to laugh or cry.

What she did do was cross to the woman and take Bobby from her. She needed to touch something that linked her to her life and not this Alice in Wonderland place she had unwillingly found herself in.

Olivia struggled to wrap her head around this latest twist, still confused about what had happened to her beautiful car. "You did this?"

"Not personally," Miss Joan answered, stretching out her words as she searched for the right ones to say next. "Bruiser did. His chew toys are leather," she explained quickly. "He likes the smell."

"He likes more than the smell," Olivia declared, clearly distressed. "He obviously likes the taste, too."

Holding Bobby to her, Olivia inspected the damage

more closely. It was as if expensive upholstery had met with the blades of a blender head-on—and come out the obvious loser.

"Bruiser likes to patrol the area," Miss Joan said haplessly. "He thinks he's keeping me safe."

Olivia stared incredulously at the woman. "And he thought my car was going to attack you?"

"I'm sorry," Miss Joan apologized. "Like I said, I'll pay for it. Shouldn't take Mick more than a week to get it fixed."

"A week?" Olivia echoed.

She didn't have a week. She barely had a couple more days. She'd taken a specific leave of absence from her firm to search for her sister and her nephew. And while the senior partners at Norvil and Tyler indicated that they valued her and viewed her as an asset to the company, Olivia was not naive. She was well aware of the way things worked. A whole slew of second-tier attorneys waited in the wings for the first glimpse of an opening. They would all be willing and eager to fill her space.

Suddenly overwhelmingly weary, Olivia felt as though the two halves of her life were on a collision course. On the one hand, she needed to be back at work, to keep building her career. On the other, she needed to be here for Tina and for Bobby. She couldn't abandon either one of them. She couldn't just pick up and leave with the baby, waiting until such time as the doctor who'd operated on Tina gave her the go-ahead to take her sister back home to Dallas. And maintaining a vigil for Tina while keeping Bobby with her came with its own set of problems as well.

Okay, first things first, she told herself. One step at a time. "I need a place to stay tonight," she said to Miss Joan.

"There's the motel on the outskirts of town," Lupe told her, coming out of the diner to join the small gathering. The few customers inside the diner were either eating or relaxing after a meal. No one was in any hurry. The regulars never were.

Miss Joan frowned at the waitress's suggestion, vetoing it.

"You don't want to go there," she said, shaking her head. "They got bugs and snakes in every room. You'll be putting the baby at risk, not to mention yourself."

Olivia shivered. She wasn't exactly open to sharing space with bugs and snakes. She began thinking that she and Bobby were going to have to spend the night in her chewed-up car—once she got the top up. *If* she could get the top up, she qualified.

"Are there any other options?" she asked.

Again, Miss Joan seemed embarrassed, as if she had once more dropped the ball. "I'd put you up, except that I'm having the house painted and I'm staying with my sister right now." Her brown eyes shifted toward Rick. "How about you, Sheriff? You've got that big ol' spare bedroom just sitting there, going to waste. You could put her and the baby up."

Oh no, Olivia thought. Staying with the sheriff was not a good idea. It was just asking for trouble and from where she stood, she had more than her share of that right now.

She shook her head, rejecting the suggestion. "I don't think—"

Miss Joan didn't let her finish. "Sure, you do," she contradicted. "The alternative's either sleeping in your car, or with vermin. You might not mind it, but you've got to think of the baby. In the motel, he could get bit. In your car, he could catch a chill. It's settled then," Miss Joan declared, seeming pleased with herself. "Why don't I put together some dinner for the two of you—on the house," she added quickly, "seeing as how Bruiser made lunch out of the inside of your car. Not that I'm trying to get out of paying for that, but dinner's the least I can do to show you how really sorry I am." With that, the woman turned on her heel and hurried back into the diner. "I'll have it ready in a jiffy," she promised.

Olivia blinked, trying to focus. She felt as if she'd just been run over by a steamroller, one that used words like "jiffy." Without realizing it, she tightened her arms around the baby, and Bobby squealed in protest. Startled, Olivia loosened her hold just enough. Sniffing, Bobby settled down.

"Look, if you don't feel comfortable about this," Rick began, choosing his words carefully, "I can ask around, see if I can find someone willing to put the two of you up."

She was beginning to feel like a charity case. She didn't want him supplicating on her behalf. If she had to make a choice, she'd rather stay with him than a stranger. At least she knew the sheriff. Sort of.

Olivia forced a smile to her lips. "I don't feel uncomfortable," she lied. And then it dawned on her. Maybe it wasn't her he was concerned about. Maybe there was a girlfriend, a lover, who wouldn't take kindly to her staying at his house.

"Unless you'd rather that we went somewhere el—"

"I'm fine with it," he told Olivia, cutting her off abruptly.

Olivia was far from convinced he meant what he said. Maybe there was a back room at the diner she and Bobby could use. They had to close down sometime, right? "You're sure?"

"I'm sure." He said it so firmly, he left no room for doubt—or argument.

"All right," she murmured, even though it was against her better judgment.

She wasn't afraid of Santiago. It was more a case of being afraid of being alone with him. Throughout this whole day, she'd felt something…something shimmering between them. Tension, electricity, attraction.

Something.

Suddenly, Olivia stifled a scream as Bobby grabbed her hair and yanked hard. Every single hair seemed to separate from her scalp. He'd managed to bring tears of pain to her eyes.

"Here, let me get that," Rick offered. Very carefully, he loosened the chubby little fingers just enough to remove the strand of hair caught in the baby's grasp. "Better?" he asked once he'd freed her hair.

"Better," she breathed. The next moment, she thrust the baby at him. "Could you hold Bobby for me for a minute? I want to get my suitcase out of the trunk."

"Sure thing." Rick took the infant from her before she could finish her question.

Bobby instantly lit up. It was not lost on Olivia. "He really seems to like you," she observed, pulling the trunk release on the driver's side floor. The trunk popped open.

"The feeling," Rick told her as he looked at the little person in his arms, "is mutual."

Rick turned so that he could watch as she took out the suitcase, then fished out the other, larger case from the inside of the car. The latter was filled with supplies she'd brought along for her nephew—disposable diapers and a few changes of clothing. She'd even packed one of the boy's toys, he noted. The woman was nothing if not prepared, an admirable quality. Along with all her other admirable qualities.

"Here," Rick said, offering the baby to her. "Why don't you take Bobby and I'll just deposit these things in my car. Along with the food," he added, seeing Miss Joan headed for them.

Olivia caught herself thinking that she could get used to this.

Immediately, she warned herself against trusting someone's kindness. Good things never lasted. The only person she could rely on was herself. She had to remember that. To think anything else was to leave herself open to disappointment and disaster. The sooner she remembered that, the better off she would be.

Chapter Ten

It looked like a home that had seen its share of happiness. Olivia felt it the moment she saw it. She didn't have to be told that this was Rick's house. She just knew.

Single story with a white stucco exterior, the house had a paint job old enough to have witnessed several winters, but not so old that it showed signs of suffering from the effects of a merciless summer sun.

When Rick pulled his car up in the driveway and turned off the ignition, Olivia hesitated about getting out. There were lights on in the house.

"Maybe you should have called ahead and checked if it was all right to bring home houseguests." She glanced into the back of the car at her nephew. Lulled by the drive, he was sound asleep. A condition subject to change at the drop of a hat. "Especially one who cries."

"You'll just have to work on that," he quipped, humor curving his mouth. And then he saw that she was serious. "And called ahead to check with who?" he asked.

A girlfriend? A wife? A friend? She shrugged, at a loss as to specifics. "With whoever's in the house."

Rick watched her. "There's no one in the house," he told her.

His sister was away at college—her last year—so there was no one to greet him when he came home at night, a fact he was acutely aware of. He was seriously thinking of getting a dog, except it wouldn't be fair to the dog to leave him alone all day. Conditions at the sheriff's office were fairly relaxed, but not enough to accommodate a dog.

Olivia got out and began to remove the infant seat restraints holding Bobby in place. Bobby continued sleeping.

She nodded toward the house. "The lights are on," she pointed out.

Was that it? He laughed, shaking his head. "Automatic timer. Makes it seem less empty when I come home."

"That bothers you? The emptiness," she added when he didn't answer. He didn't strike her as the lonely type.

"Sometimes," he allowed. He took out the cooler filled with baby bottles and formula that she'd transferred into his vehicle, as well as her suitcase. "My sister lives here when she's not away at college. After an entire summer of Mona's chatter, the house feels unnaturally quiet when she's gone."

"You get along with your sister?" she asked, following him to the front door.

"Better now that she's outgrown her bratty stage," he quipped.

He paused to unlock the front door, then picked up the cooler and suitcase again, only to park both just inside the door. Rick waited as she looked around, wondering what she thought of his home. He assumed that she was accustomed to fancier digs, but this suited him. Even though he would most likely take that job in Dallas, this would always be home to him.

"Let me show you to your room," he offered.

He led Olivia and the baby down a very short hall. He opened the door to the first room on the left. It was a very feminine bedroom. The double bed had a canopy overhead. The canopy matched the white eyelet bedspread which, in turn, matched the shams on the pillows.

Bobby began to stir. She automatically started to sway, attempting to lull him back to sleep. "Let me guess, this is your sister's room?" Olivia didn't exactly like the idea of invading someone else's space, even if they weren't there to witness it.

"No, my grandmother's." He looked at her, amused. So far, both guesses she'd made about the house had been wrong. "You're not very good at this game, are you, Olivia?"

Because he was putting them up, she bit back the first retort that rose to her lips. Instead, she looked around again. He'd said that no one was home. That didn't mean that someone wasn't due back. "Your grandmother, where is she?"

A fond look came into his eyes. "Probably bossing the angels around, telling them how to play their harps if I know her."

"Then she's—?"

"Yes," Rick answered quickly, cutting her short before she could say the word he really didn't care to hear.

"I'm sorry."

"Yeah, so was I." His grandmother had been gruff and strict, but both he and his sister knew she loved them. That was never in question. "This is her house. She left it to me and to Mona. Abuelita said it was all she could give us." There was irony in his smile. "She didn't realize that she'd given us so much more than just a building. She gave us a home."

Aware that his voice had become softer when he spoke about the old woman, Rick cleared his throat, as if that could erase outward signs of sentiment. He became all business.

"Listen, I might be able to find Mona's old playpen in the attic. It would give you someplace to put your nephew when he's sleeping." He nodded over toward the bed. "That way you don't have to worry about him rolling off and hurting himself."

He really was more thoughtful than she'd given him credit for, she thought, impressed.

"Thank you," she murmured. If there was a playpen in the attic, they had to have lived in the house a long time. "How long have you and your sister lived here?"

"Mona was six when my grandmother took us in. I was eleven, but she took care of us off and on—mostly on—right from the beginning." His eyes met hers. "Why?"

"Just curious," she answered evasively. It occurred to her that she was asking too many personal questions.

Olivia had a feeling he felt the same way when he replied, "Uh-huh."

When she turned to ask him what he meant by that, Rick had already left the room. A couple of minutes later, she could hear the sheriff walking around in the attic, just above her head.

That was when Bobby woke up fully and began to fuss. Like any three-month-old who hadn't eaten in a couple of hours, he was hungry. He let her know the only way he knew how. He cried.

"Message delivered, loud and clear," she assured him. The next moment, she began to sing softly, hoping to distract him. She made her way back to the front of the house and the cooler. Bending down carefully, still singing, she extracted a bottle. "Now all I need to do is find a microwave," she told her nephew. Bobby cried again. "You don't want to know the logistics, you just want your bottle, right?"

She shifted the baby to her other side, took the bottle and went in search of the kitchen.

It wasn't much of a search. By the time Rick came back downstairs, carrying the slightly scarred playpen— folded in fourths—in his hands, she had just finished warming Bobby's bottle and was testing its warmth on the inside of her wrist.

"I see you found the kitchen," he noted.

"Wasn't hard. It was the only room with a stove," she cracked. Sitting down with the baby, she began feeding him. "And you found the playpen."

He leaned the playpen against a wall and went to the sink to retrieve a dish towel. After running water over it, he crossed back to the playpen.

"It's a bit dusty," he told her, "but nothing a little water won't fix. There's even a mattress for it." That, too, was folded in fourths inside the playpen. "It's kind of thin," he admitted, "but I can fold up a couple of blankets and put them on top of it. That should keep him comfortable."

Bobby made greedy sucking noises as he ate. She smiled at him. She'd never thought about having children—taking care of Tina had filled that void, or so she thought. But Bobby had stirred things up, made longings emerge. Longings that probably didn't have a chance in hell of being fulfilled. That didn't make them any less intense.

"Why are you going to all this trouble?" she asked Rick suddenly. After all, they were nothing to him.

"Because he needs a place to sleep. And so do you," he added. "And Miss Joan was right, that motel is too vermin infested. You'd probably catch something, sleeping there."

It wasn't that she wasn't grateful, she was just trying to understand. "But we're perfect strangers."

One side of his mouth rose a little higher than the other, giving him an oddly endearing appearance that instantly shot a salvo through her gut. She tried not to notice, but it was too late.

"I don't know about perfect," Rick said, "but as for being a stranger, my grandmother always said that a stranger was just a friend you haven't made yet." And then he laughed quietly. "Of course, she said it in Spanish, but I think the translation might be lost on you."

Olivia vaguely recalled taking Spanish in high school, but right now, that seemed like another lifetime. Her sense of competition goaded her to answer him in Spanish, some small, trite phrase she could fit her tongue around. But with her luck, he'd think that she was fluent and start rattling off at a mile a minute. If that happened, she'd only be able to marginally follow maybe a few key words. And maybe not even that. She didn't want to amuse him, she wanted to impress him.

Why? In a couple of days, you're never going to see him again. Why does impressing him matter?

She didn't know why, it just did.

"You're right," she agreed, "it would be. I only remember a few words in Spanish, none of which would work their way into a regular conversation."

She had him wondering what those words were.

Olivia focused her attention on her nephew. The greediness had abated and his pace had slowed. He'd only consumed half his bottle. Thinking it best not to force him to drink any more, Olivia placed the bottle on the table and then lifted Bobby up, placing the infant against her shoulder. In a routine that had become second nature to her, especially in the middle of the night, she began patting the baby's back, coaxing a burp from him.

For once, the burp didn't come with a soggy deposit of formula on her shoulder. The small eyes drifted shut and he dozed off again. With any luck, she would be able to put him down for a few hours.

Very softly, she tiptoed back into the bedroom where Rick had put the playpen. She laid her nephew down very carefully, afraid of waking him up. She needn't have worried. Tonight, he slept like a rock. She thanked God for small favors.

She paused over the playpen for a moment longer, looking down at this small, perfect human being. For the most part, Bobby led an uneventful life and right now, she had to admit she envied him for it. Her own life seemed to be going at ninety miles an hour with no signs of slowing down.

As she turned away from the playpen she almost walked right into Rick, who was standing in the door-way observing her. He stepped back at the last minute, preventing a collision.

How was it, she wondered, that she could feel the heat radiating from his body? Feel it against her own skin.

"I'm going to warm up a little of what Miss Joan sent over. You interested?" he asked.

Yes, she was interested. Definitely interested. But not in anything that could be warmed up on a plate. The thought had come at her from left field, startling her. She shook her head, trying to extinguish the thought.

"No?" he questioned when she simply shook her head.

That hadn't been to answer him, that was to clear her head. "No—yes. A little," she qualified.

"That wasn't a multiple-choice question." He studied her for a minute. "You okay?"

"Yes," she answered a tad too quickly. "Just punchy, I think. I'm going to stay here a few minutes longer, just to make sure he stays asleep."

"Okay."

As he walked out of the room, heading for the kitchen, he could hear her singing softly under her breath. Some sort of lullaby, he guessed.

She had a nice voice.

RICK HAD JUST FINISHED heating up the food and putting it on the table when Olivia walked into the kitchen. "He still asleep?" he asked.

Just for a moment, she'd debated using Bobby as an excuse, as a shield to hide behind. But she refused to behave like a coward. What was she afraid of? Eating? Sitting opposite a good-looking man and talking? It sounded very silly, putting it that way.

"Still asleep," she echoed. "For now." She took a deep breath and smiled. "Smells good."

"I added a few things," he confessed. That was when she noticed a collection of small jars of herbs and spices scattered along the counter like partying soldiers. "We can eat in the kitchen, or on the patio. It's fairly warm tonight."

And there was a blanket of stars out tonight. She'd noticed that when she'd gotten out of the car. The thought of sitting with him in such a blatantly romantic setting made her feel uneasy.

She seized the first excuse she could think of. "I think we should stay in the kitchen. I won't be able to hear Bobby if he cries if we're outside."

"Good point. Kitchen it is." He gestured toward the table. "Have a seat."

She sank down in the closest chair. Picking up a fork, she took a tentative bite of what he'd prepared. And then another, and another. The food tasted progressively better with each bite she took.

Olivia glanced over to the counter beside the stove. More than a few containers had been left out. She recalled Rick telling her that his grandmother had taught him how to cook.

Good-looking, sensitive and he knew how to cook. As far as she could see, that made him a triple threat and damn near perfect.

There had to be something wrong with Rick. What was the deal breaker here? Was the man a closet serial killer? As she slanted a look at him, she had a pretty good feeling that wasn't it.

Rick could feel her eyes on him. Was she trying to find a polite way to tell him that she didn't like his augmentations to the meal?

Rather than speculate, he asked. "What?"

"Why aren't you married?"

He didn't know what he expected her to say, or ask, but this didn't even remotely come close. But two could play at this game. "Why aren't you?"

A fair question, she supposed. She told him what she told herself. "I've been too busy."

Rick laughed shortly. "Right. The weight-of-the-world-on-your-shoulders thing."

Just what was he implying? That she was using her busy schedule as an excuse not to get into any serious relationships?

Well, aren't you?

Lots of people had thriving careers and still had the wherewithal and time to find love. She didn't have a relationship because she was afraid. Afraid of losing someone else the way she'd lost her parents. Without any warning. In the blink of an eye. To lose a spouse like that, someone you loved with your whole being, would be completely devastating. She honestly didn't know if she could survive that. The only solution was not to put herself in that position in the first place. If she kept out of the minefield, she wouldn't run the risk of blowing up.

"Well, you certainly can't use that excuse," she retorted defensively. Then she suggested, with a trace of sarcasm, "How about the other tried and true one? The one that goes 'I never met the right girl'?"

Rick pulled his shoulders back. She'd struck a nerve without realizing it. If he flippantly agreed just to terminate this line of dialogue, it would be dishonoring Alycia's memory. Dishonoring it because she *had* been the right girl. And he would have been happy spending the rest of his life loving her.

Taking a deep breath, his eyes met hers. "Oh, I met her all right."

"And? What happened?"

When he spoke, his voice was completely devoid of emotion. Because he couldn't allow himself to feel anything. It hurt too much.

"She died."

For a moment, Olivia thought he was pulling her leg. But then she looked into his eyes and knew that he wasn't. He was serious, and she felt terrible. The man had voluntarily acted as her chauffeur, driving her to the hospital when he didn't have to. He'd literally taken her and Bobby in and she was repaying him by callously digging up memories best left untouched. Not once but twice.

What was the matter with her?

She knew she should be apologizing, backing away from the painful subject as quickly as she could. That was the way she normally handled an uncomfortable situation.

That wasn't the way she handled it now.

All sorts of questions buzzed in her head, looking for answers. "What was her name?"

"Alycia."

"Alycia," she repeated. "That's a beautiful name."

The smile was sad. "She was a beautiful woman."

An emotion she seldom experienced reared its head. Jealous. She was jealous.

How could she be feeling jealous? Jealous of a dead woman?

Because no one had ever felt that way about her; no one had ever said her name with such sorrow echoing in his voice.

Olivia pressed her lips together, her mind ordering her to drop the subject. She didn't listen, of course. Instead, she heard herself asking, "What happened to her?" And for the life of her, she wouldn't have been able to explain why she was asking. She just needed to know.

He recited the circumstances to her the way he had to her parents, struggling to distance himself from the words. "One of those cross-country moving vans lost control and jackknifed on the highway, crushing her car. Doctor said she died instantly."

How devastatingly awful for him. She felt his pain. Felt that terrible hole widening in her gut. "I don't know what to say."

He shrugged carelessly, looking away. "Nothing to say."

The ensuing silence seemed to separate them.

This would have been a good time for Bobby to wake up crying. But he didn't wake up. He continued sleeping. "Is it true?" she asked.

"Is what true?"

"That saying about it being better to have loved and

lost than never to have loved at all." She had no idea why it was suddenly important for her to know.

"You mean if I had a choice between losing her and never having had her at all, which would I pick?" She nodded in response. "That's easy. I'm glad I had her for whatever short time we shared together."

It made her realize how empty her own life was, despite the turmoil and the breakneck pace she kept. The thought negated her tired feeling and made her restless instead.

"Let me get the dishes for you," she offered. She needed to do something with her hands.

"No need," he told her. "I usually just stack them in the sink until I run out of plates and glasses. I've got a few days to go."

"I can't sleep with dirty dishes in the sink," she said.

As she reached for his plate, he put his hand out to stop her and nearly wound up knocking over his glass. He made a grab for it and so did she. The result was that her fingers went around the glass and his went around her hand.

Something basic and raw, and very, very vulnerable telegraphed itself back and forth between them.

It was hard to pinpoint the source, whether it originated with her, or with him. The only thing that was clear was what pulsated between them. Waiting for a chance to explode.

Chapter Eleven

For one isolated, tense moment, Olivia was almost certain that the man was going to kiss her. And, if she was being honest with herself, *hoped* he would kiss her.

But the moment slowly passed and nothing happened.

Embarrassed and determined not to show it, Olivia cleared her throat and nodded toward the glass that they were both keeping upright. "I think you can let go. I've got it."

"Yes," Rick agreed quietly, the timbre of his voice softly slipping along her skin, sending her body temperature up by several degrees, "you do."

The erratic electricity rushing up and down her spine made her oblivious to everything else in the room.

Everything but Rick.

She couldn't help wondering if this man had a clue as to how sexy he was, and that he just seemed to radiate sensual appeal simply by breathing. He couldn't be oblivious to it, but he acted as if he didn't realize that he was tall, dark and bone-meltingly handsome.

Were the women in this town blind?

One by one, his fingers left her hand. She became

aware of the fact that she'd stopped breathing for the duration of the contact.

"Maybe you're right about those dishes," Olivia murmured, tearing her eyes away from his. "Maybe I'd better get to bed and get some rest. It's been a very long day and there's no telling how long Bobby's going to be asleep."

Rick nodded, as if he didn't see through the thin excuse. As if he didn't know that she was running for dear life, running from something that had flared to life. Something that, given the present situation, had absolutely no chance of longevity.

"See you in the morning," he said.

"Right."

Instantly on her feet, Olivia got out of the kitchen—and away from him—as fast as possible without running. She needed to get away before she regretted her actions and consequently had him thinking she was the kind of woman she wasn't. The kind of woman who enjoyed having casual, fleeting hookups.

She wasn't that kind of a woman.

Olivia couldn't remember the last time she'd been alone with a man who wasn't engaged in giving her a deposition.

Get a grip, she silently lectured, leaning against the bedroom door she'd just closed.

Lectures not withstanding, it took a while for her heart to settle down and stop pounding.

RICK HAD ALWAYS THOUGHT of himself as a light sleeper. But apparently, there was light and then there was *light*. Although he thought he'd been listening for the baby's cries, when morning broke he hadn't heard any sounds coming from his miniature houseguest—or the baby's aunt.

There was no other reason why, when he made his way to the kitchen, Rick was caught by surprise when he found her in the room ahead of him.

But there she was, in the center of a homey scene that looked straight out of some Family Channel Christmas celebration. She was making breakfast with the scent of fresh brewed coffee—strong, just the way he liked it—filling the air, along with other delicious aromas.

What really completed the picture for him was Olivia, standing there with her hair down about her shoulders. She looked younger, softer. Approachable. And damn embraceable.

Shoving his hands into the pockets of his jeans, Rick masked his surprise. "You cook?" It turned out he wasn't the only one who was surprised that morning.

When Olivia glanced over her shoulder at him, about to confirm his query, she almost dropped the spatula. She *did* drop her jaw. Last night, she hadn't thought it was humanly possible for Sheriff Enrique Santiago to look any sexier than he did.

But she was wrong.

Barefoot and with his hair tousled, he was sexier than any living creature had a right to be. Especially since he'd neglected to button the shirt he'd carelessly thrown on. It hung open, testifying to the fact that the good sheriff was either the recipient of some incredibly fantastic genes from his family tree, or that he worked out religiously. She could count all his rigidly displayed abdominal muscles.

It took her too long to find her tongue, although she congratulated herself for not swallowing it.

"I cook," she finally replied in a voice that was only a shade less than breathless.

Turning away because she was afraid of melting on the spot, Olivia drew in a long breath and tried to access her brain.

Her first attempt failed.

This would have been a good time for Bobby to start crying, rescuing her from an awkward moment. She glanced over to where she'd relocated the playpen. But the little boy had suddenly developed an overwhelming fascination with his hands, which he held up in the air and twisted in every conceivable direction, obviously marveling at their dexterity by cooing and gurgling.

With no small relief, Olivia could feel her brain function again. "I thought that making you breakfast was the very least I could do to say thank you for putting us up like this." She hadn't cooked in years, not once there'd been enough money for takeout from one of the better Dallas restaurants, but, like riding a bike, it had come back to her.

"Nothing to thank me for," Rick assured her, taking a seat. She placed a steaming cup of black coffee before him. He smiled appreciatively. The aroma was enough to kick-start his day and get him going. "The room was there whether or not you used it." He took a slow sip, letting the inky liquid wind its way through him, waking up every cell it came in contact with. "You sleep well?" he asked her.

She had slept like a woman anticipating an earthquake, but no way could she have admitted that and not had him asking embarrassing questions. "I have a lot on my mind and Bobby was restless, but under the circumstances, yes, I think I slept pretty well."

The sheriff's deep green eyes held hers for a moment and she had the impression that she hadn't fooled him at all, but that could have been her own paranoia.

Turning back to the stove, Olivia quickly slid the omelet and the warm slice of Texas toast from the griddle onto a plate and placed the latter before him next to his coffee cup.

He sampled the omelet first. The next moment, he was smiling and nodding his approval. "This is really good. I didn't think you knew how to cook," he confessed. She hadn't struck him as the type who would have taken the time to learn.

They were both guilty of typecasting each other, she thought, amused.

"Had to," she told him. "It's a lot cheaper than takeout and when you're on a tight budget, every penny counts." That he seemed to understand. "These days I don't have to worry about living from paycheck to paycheck. But that doesn't mean I can't whip something up if I have to. I actually like cooking."

"Lucky for me I got to be around when you started whipping," Rick commented, doing justice to the serving she'd given him. He was almost half finished. "This is *really* good."

Maybe it had something to do with having all her nerve endings so close to the surface. Whatever the reason, Olivia hadn't thought a simple compliment could please her so much. But it did.

"Thank you."

"Aren't you going to have any?"

"I never seem to be able to eat anything I make, at least, not until it reaches the leftover stage." She'd always cooked for Tina and wound up nibbling a little of the meal later on.

"That would explain the killer figure," he observed, "but you really should have something."

She barely heard the second part of his statement. The first had caught her up short, even though he'd uttered it as if it was just a throwaway line. And telling herself that he probably handed out kind words a lot more than he handed out tickets didn't temper the effect the compliment had on her. For a moment, she reveled in the words, smiling, Olivia had no doubt, like some village idiot.

"I'll have some coffee," she said, taking down another cup from the cupboard and filling it three-quarters of the way up.

"That'll put meat on your bones," he quipped.

She didn't have to look at Rick to know that he was grinning. She could hear it in his voice. Was he teasing her, or being sarcastic? And why should it matter either way? Once Tina was conscious, she was out of here. More than likely, she'd never see Santiago again.

Even so, she couldn't let his comment go. "Do I look that skinny to you?"

She wasn't fishing for another compliment, but it had been a long while since she'd actually looked at her reflection and maybe she'd lost touch with the woman she had become. Her life, in the past year, had been one great big blur of briefs, trials—and coming to grips with Tina getting pregnant and giving birth to Bobby.

Having Don in the mix hadn't exactly helped with clarity, either.

"No," Rick replied honestly. "You don't. But you will if you just run on liquids. You really should eat something. Didn't your mother ever tell you that breakfast was the most important meal of the day?"

"I vaguely recall something like that," she admitted. "Point noted." She nodded her head as she held the steaming cup of black coffee with both hands, drawing in comfort from the heat.

Olivia glanced over his shoulder and out the window. The world outside hadn't lightened up any and, at this hour, it should have. Instead, it was growing progressively darker.

"Looks like rain," she observed.

There was concern in her voice. He knew what she was thinking. That if it rained, he might use that as an excuse not to take her back to the hospital. She needn't have worried. He'd never seen rain as a deterrent.

"The crops could do with some rain," he told her. "Ground's been getting parched."

She took a breath, inching toward her subject slowly. She needed him so she was careful not to be too blunt. "Do you have flash floods around here?"

"Don't worry, I'll take you back up. Barring a daring bank robbery taking place here, of course."

Rick sounded so serious, it took her a moment to realize he was kidding.

And then she smiled. "I take it you don't have robberies out here."

"Oh, every once in a while, theft does rear its head. Usually it's some school kid being threatened by the class bully for his lunch money or something along those lines. Most of the time, though, Forever's pretty much safe as safe can be." He was rather proud of that, even though Forever's tranquility added to his general boredom and ultimately had caused him to apply to the Dallas PD.

Can't have it both ways, Santiago, he silently lectured. *Either be content with the peace or go where the action is.*

The baby began to fuss. Her rest period over, Olivia was on her feet in an instant. "He wants his bottle," she said.

In anticipation of Bobby's next feeding—she'd already updated a schedule for the infant—she'd prepared the bottle just before Rick had walked into the kitchen. After taking Bobby out of the playpen, she sat down and fed him.

Rick was surprised that watching her with the baby could stir such warm feelings within him. After all, neither one was anything to him. There was no reason for him to be experiencing this kind of a reaction.

And yet, he was.

Further proof, he decided, that he really did need a change. To move on and find a new place for himself. A new, rewarding place. Who knew what that would bring with it?

MICK HENLEY CUT his long weekend short and returned a day early, grumbling to anyone within earshot that it was raining "cats and dogs" at his favorite fishing hole some fifty miles southeast of Forever. Being

soaked to the skin clearly took away some of the pleasure generated by pitting himself against nature.

On his stop by the diner for some much needed
hot coffee, Mick was informed by Miss Joan that the
"chewed up, overpriced piece of machinery sittin'" outside" her place was in desperate need of his skills.

Those were the words he used when he showed up on
Rick's doorstep that morning just as Rick was finishing
up his breakfast.

"Miss Joan said that the lady who's got the keys to
that sorry vehicle's staying here," said the tall, almost
painfully thin mechanic. He raised himself up on his
toes in order to peer into the sheriff's house, most likely
to see if he could spot the woman in question. Rick was
six-two, but Henley was approximately two inches taller,
seeming even taller because he was so rail-thin.

Drawn by the sound of voices, Olivia came up behind
Rick, holding Bobby in her arms. She heard the stranger's last sentence.

"It won't start," she told the mechanic. She looked at
him a little uncertainly. This was the town mechanic?
The man looked more like a wild-eyed prophet out of
some poorly cast movie set in biblical times. All he
needed was a flowing robe and rope sandals to go with
his long, straggly gray hair and the three-day stubble
on his gaunt face.

"So Miss Joan tells me. She also tells me that Bruiser
used your car as a big teething ring." He laughed shortly.
The noise sounded more like a cackle to Olivia. "I always
did say that dog was a decent judge of machinery."

She didn't feel overly optimistic about leaving her
car's fate in the hands of a mechanic who took his lead

from a dog, but, since Henley was the only mechanic in town, she had no choice.

"Do you think that you can fix the problem?" she asked, trying to sound as upbeat as she could.

"Can't rightly say," he told her honestly. "Haven't figured out what the problem is yet. Well, since I ain't got nothing else to do, I'll tow your car to my garage and have a look-see." About to leave, he paused. "You got the keys?"

"Not on me, but I'll go get them," she said, debating whether she should add, "don't go anywhere," or if that was understood. The man didn't seem overly bright, but she decided not to state the obvious. She was counting on Rick to keep the man there until she retrieved the car keys. "I'll be just a minute," she promised.

With that, Olivia hurried off to the bedroom, where she'd left her purse. She was back within moments. Bobby gurgled, obviously enjoying the quick sprint to the rear of the house and back.

Returning, she was just in time to see the semi-amused, utterly envious look that the older mechanic was giving Rick. Curious, she instinctively knew to keep her question to herself.

"Here they are," she said, rejoining the two men. She held out the car keys to Henley.

Long, sun-browned and permanently stained fingers wrapped themselves around the keys. Henley nodded. "We'll talk again," he promised, taking his leave.

About the car, or about something else? An uneasy feeling slid up and down her spine. But then, if the old man had meant anything sinister, Rick would have called him out on it, right? The latter was the law around here, she reminded herself, for whatever that was worth.

She was beginning to feel as if she'd gotten trapped in an episode of *The Twilight Zone.* How else could she explain this sudden, strong attraction for Rick? It just wasn't like her and yet, every time she came within close proximity of the man, her system suddenly and loudly declared: Go!

"And he's the only mechanic in town?" she questioned Rick again, watching Henley's back as he retreated to his vehicle, a fifteen-year-old truck that had definitely seen better days.

"Yes." Rick added for her benefit, "Don't worry, Mick's good at what he does."

"I certainly hope so," Olivia murmured. Any further exchange was curtailed as they both became aware of the fact that Bobby had pungently recycled his breakfast. "I'd better go change him," she said with a sigh.

"Not a bad idea," Rick agreed as she turned to hurry back to the bedroom.

WHEN RICK TOOK her to the hospital later that day, her hopes that Tina had regained consciousness quickly died. Her sister was no better. On the bright side, the surgeon told her, when she caught up to him, that Tina was no worse, either.

"You've got to understand, Ms. Blayne," he told her, "This is a process that doesn't have a specific timetable. It doesn't punch a time clock that says it'll be gone in a certain amount of hours or days. We just have to wait and see how she responds. And you're going to have to stay patient," he added.

That was easy for the doctor to say. His whole life was here. He didn't have a job waiting for him back in Dallas. A job that came with a very impatient boss who, when she'd asked for some time off, had looked as if it physically pained him to give her even a short leave of absence.

A leave of absence that might not be nearly long enough.

She would have to call Norvil tomorrow to request an extension. She definitely wasn't looking forward to that. All things considered, she would rather go before Susan Reems, known as the district's "hanging judge" to plead a case rather than ask Harris Norvil for a favor.

She stayed with Tina for several hours, talking to her, reading to her, hoping to bring her sister around, if only just a little.

But nothing changed and, finally, she asked Rick to take her back to Forever.

"At least there was no bad news," Rick said as they drove back, trying to be encouraging. And he was right, she thought. Things could have been a lot worse.

The bad news waited for them once they got back to Forever. They stopped to pick up the baby at the diner and returned to Rick's house. No sooner did they walk through the door than the phone rang.

"It's for you," Rick said, holding out the receiver. "It's Mick. Here, I'll take the baby," he offered, trading her the receiver for the infant.

She had a bad feeling about this. "Hello?"

Mick started talking immediately. "It ain't a death sentence or nothing like that," he assured her. "But your car needs parts I don't carry—don't usually work on fancy, pricey cars—but I can order them. Shouldn't be but a couple of days—"

"A couple of days?" she echoed. She'd hoped it was something simple, like a new battery.

"If we're lucky," Henley tacked on. "Now, you want me to send for 'em, or just forget the whole thing?"

That wasn't an option and she had a feeling this skinny highwayman knew it. "Send for them," she instructed, biting back a sigh.

"First thing in the morning," he promised.

The connection went dead. She stood there holding the receiver, fighting the urge to throw it across the room. Olivia hung it up instead.

She went in search of Bobby and found him in the guest room. Rick was playing peekaboo with him and Bobby was laughing a funny belly laugh that had already become part of his personality.

Standing there, watching them for a couple of minutes, she could feel the knot in her stomach unclenching. The child wasn't really hers. Neither was the man. But it didn't matter. For one isolated moment in time, she looked upon it as a family scene, something she was part of by virtue of simply *being* there and it made her feel good.

She found that she could even smile.

Chapter Twelve

For the next three days, as the threat of rain hung in the air, so prevalent that Olivia could almost taste the drops, the sheriff-with-the-heart-of-gold drove her to see her sister every morning and then drove her back to Forever and her nephew at the end of the day. In between, Rick would disappear, leaving her to stay with her sister and pray for a miracle as she kept up almost a steady stream of conversation, interspersed with reading the local newspaper out loud to Tina.

It made no difference.

Tina remained in a coma, out of reach. It was getting harder and harder to see her sister that way.

As her mind searched for positive things to dwell on, Olivia began to wonder where Rick went during the day after he left her at the hospital. Was he visiting friends he knew in town? Going to the movies? What?

When he came to Tina's room to pick her up the evening of the third day, Olivia decided to ask him outright. She knew that he had every right to his privacy and she had no right to pry.

But knowing that didn't diminish her curiosity.

However, before she could open her mouth to ask,

Rick handed her an umbrella. That was when she noticed that his hat and jacket were wet. Not damp from accumulated drizzle, but wet, *really* wet.

"You're going to need this," he told her. "It's raining like there's no tomorrow." The sheriff glanced over Olivia's shoulder at the unconscious young woman in the bed, then back at her. "No change?"

"No change." God, but she hated the sound of those words. They were the same two words the nurses told her every morning as she walked into the ICU, asking how Tina was doing.

Rick gave her an encouraging smile as he led the way toward the front entrance. "Maybe tomorrow."

"Yes, maybe tomorrow," Olivia echoed, wishing she could actually believe that.

Whether Tina regained consciousness or not, once her car was back among the running, she was going back to Dallas to talk to their family physician to find out what it took to get Tina airlifted from Pine Ridge Memorial and brought to Parkland Memorial Hospital, one of the outstanding hospitals in the state. The doctors there must be able to bring Tina around. Parkland Memorial attracted a more gifted class of surgeon, she thought, tamping down the desperate feeling within her.

It wasn't raining when she walked through the door and went outside. It was pouring. Relentlessly.

"Here, take this," Rick said, opening the umbrella and thrusting it into her hand. Before she could protest that he needed it more than she did, he was gone, weaving through the parking lot to retrieve his vehicle.

The wind came from all angles, driving the rain almost at a slant on one side, then shifting positions and sending it lashing at her from the other side. She found herself shifting the umbrella from one side to the other in an attempt to keep at least semidry.

It was a losing battle.

When he drove the car up to the hospital's front entrance several minutes later, she saw once again that Rick looked absolutely soaked to the bone. Shutting the umbrella as swiftly as she could, she dived into the front passenger seat and quickly shut the door. Despite her efforts, she was almost as wet as Rick.

"Why didn't you take the umbrella?" she asked.

The shrug was dismissive and careless. "It would have just held me up."

It was a lie and they both knew it. He'd left it with her in hopes that it would keep her relatively dry. Apparently chivalry was not dead, at least not in Forever, Texas. She didn't realize she was smiling.

Shifting in her seat and looking at his profile, she could barely make it out in the encroaching darkness and rain. "Where do you go every day?"

That struck him as an odd question. The most logical answer would have been to say "to Pine Ridge," but she wasn't simpleminded. He could tell that she assumed he didn't hang around town.

"When?"

"When you drop me off at the hospital. You never stay," she pointed out, not that he was under any obligation to stay with her. "Do you go visit friends, or…?" She let her voice trail off, waiting for him to fill in the blank.

"Or…" Rick responded, his lips curving in amusement.

Reaching over to the side, he turned on the rear window defroster and switched on the window defogger.

The windshield was clouding up. Impatient, he wiped the mist away with the palm of his hand. It didn't exactly improve visibility.

"Or," she repeated. "And that would be?" Olivia pressed, waiting.

"I go back to Forever and deal with whatever comes up during the day," he told her simply.

The heater wasn't helping all that much. Visibility was going from bad to worse. He slowed the car down to a crawl.

She must have missed something, Olivia thought. Good Samaritans were only found in Bible passages and movies of the week. "You drive all the way over here, drop me off then drive back and in the evening you repeat the whole process all over again?"

He slanted her an amused look, sparing only a second. The road needed his undivided attention. "Nothing gets by you, does it?"

"Why?"

"Why doesn't anything get by you?" he speculated as to the nature of her question. "If I had to guess, I'd say it's because you're sharp."

She wanted answers. She desperately wanted clarity for a change. And he was having fun at her expense. "Don't mock me, Rick, you know what I mean. Why are you going out of your way like this for me?"

He would have thought that it was evident. But then, life in a large city tended to make people suspicious of random acts of kindness. He spelled it out for her.

"Because your car's dead in Mick Henley's garage and your sister's in a coma in Pine Ridge Memorial and you have no way to get there," he said.

"Yes, but none of that is your problem. It's mine."

"While you're in my town, I see it differently."

Olivia watched him for a long moment as the windshield wipers rhythmically dueled with the wind-driven rain that crashed against the windshield. They were equally matched.

"Thank you," she finally managed to say. "I don't know if I remembered to tell you, but I'm very grateful to you for everything you've done for Bobby and me—and my sister."

Taking credit always made him feel awkward. Taking credit that wasn't due him only made it that much worse. "Didn't do anything for your sister except manage to locate her," he said.

He was taking modesty to a whole new level. The people she associated with in the firm would have torn him apart in a matter of moments. "But don't you understand? That was the important part. I wouldn't have found Tina if not for you."

"You would have found her," he guaranteed. "You're too stubborn not to."

Whatever she was going to say in response was swallowed up as they suddenly hit what felt like a giant pothole or, in this case, just a plain hole in the ground. The car listed to the right, her side dropping about half a foot. Olivia screamed as she slammed against the door.

"We're fine, we'll be fine," Rick insisted, raising his voice above the howl of the wind so that she could hear him.

His forearms strained and then ached as he hung on to the steering wheel, fighting for control of the vehicle.

It swerved, sliding first one way, then the other as he tried to compensate.

Struggling, he finally managed to get them beyond the sinkhole and to the side of the road. He pulled over and stopped to catch his breath.

"Do you charge extra for that?" Olivia quipped, trying to sound unfazed as she waited for her heart to stop racing.

"No extra charge," he told her.

The rain continued to get worse as they drove on. Rick began to talk, trying to take her mind off what was going on beyond the windshield, but it was futile. Visibility had gone to practically zero.

He blew out a long breath. "I think we're going to have to stop somewhere for the night. If the rain keeps up like this, I might wind up driving off the road again, or into some swollen creek."

As it was, the rain was seeping into the car via the doors. The floor had already accumulated half an inch of water and it promised to only get worse.

"*Is* there anywhere out here to stop?" Olivia asked skeptically. She didn't remember seeing a hotel.

Rick glanced at the car's navigational system. For now, it was still working, but he didn't know how much longer he was going to be able to say that. He hit the square that said "hotels." Only one name and address popped up. It barely qualified.

"There's this run-down motel about two miles from here. It doesn't look like much, but the rooms have got roofs and it's a place to stay dry while waiting for the storm to break, or for morning, whichever comes first." He glanced in her direction. "From the looks of it, some

of the roads going back home are going to be flooded.
They tend to flood when it really rains hard," he explained, then began to drive again, going very slowly.
"Staying at The Sunshine Inn's going to be our best
bet."

"IF THIS IS THE BEST BET, I'd hate to see the worst,"
Olivia commented some twenty minutes later, after she'd
called Miss Joan to explain that they were temporarily
delayed until morning and the desk clerk, a tired little
man with sleepy eyes, had handed them the keys to the
last available vacant room. According to what he told
them, stranded travelers had flocked to the motel, the
only port in the storm for miles around. His drooping
eyelids covered eyes that came close to lighting up as
he referred to the fact that this was the first time since
he had taken over as manager that every room in the
motel was rented.

The last available vacant room was the picture of
neglect. The first thing Olivia noticed was the dust. It
had gathered and formed a thin layer across the scarred
dark bureau and on both the head and footboards of the
double bed.

The bed was the second thing she noticed. There was
only one.

And there were two of them.

Rick saw the concern on her face as she regarded
the bed. "Don't worry, I'll take the floor," he told her.
Since there was no sofa or even an upholstered chair in
the room, that left only the floor for him to stretch out
on. He supposed that it was a step up from camping.

Olivia was shaking her head. "No, that's not fair," she

told him. "I've put you out enough. You take the bed, I'll take the floor." It was the only decent thing to do, she thought.

The threadbare carpet was peeling back in places and looked far from sanitary. The bed at least appeared clean, Rick judged.

"Look, we're both adults. No reason we can't share a bed," he told her. He saw the leery expression in her eyes. "One of us stays under the covers, the other sleeps on top of them. Good enough?" he asked.

If she protested, she knew he was going to think that sex was foremost on her mind and it wasn't—at least, not exactly. Left with no choice, Olivia nodded, and echoed, "Good enough," and went to see how bad the bathroom was.

She discovered that it was surprisingly clean, under the circumstances. There was even a set of bath towels that looked as if they'd been recently purchased. The pile still felt relatively fluffy.

"I'm going to take a quick shower," she said, sticking her head out of the bathroom. "Unless you want to go first."

He declined, saying, "I take my showers in the morning."

Ordinarily, so did she, but she was tense and wet from the rain. Knots the size of small boulders resided in her shoulders and she hoped a hot shower would help undo them.

"I'll be right out," she promised.

"Take your time. We're not going anywhere," he answered.

Olivia went in and closed the bathroom door. He

heard the click as she turned the lock. Definitely not a trusting woman, he thought. And in this case, maybe it was just as well. She surely represented temptation. His reaction to her all along had been a surprise to him. He hadn't been more than fleetingly attracted to a woman since he'd lost Alycia. And he *meant* fleetingly. As in a matter of minutes at best.

This, he had to admit, was something different. So having a locked door between them when she was showering wasn't the worst idea.

Looking for a diversion, Rick turned on the antiquated TV set that just barely fit on the wobbly cart. As he flipped from one channel to another, he found himself watching either static or snow. Or nothing. Apparently the weather had dealt a fatal blow to the reception in the area. Bracing himself for a long, drawn-out evening, he shut off the TV.

Just in time to hear the bloodcurdling scream coming from the bathroom.

Olivia.

He had his gun out immediately.

"Olivia, are you all right?" he shouted through the door.

When all he got was another scream in reply, he tried the doorknob. It wouldn't give. But the door itself was just barely mounted in its frame, a victim of age and time and perhaps a few rowdy parties. Rick kicked it in on his first try.

The water in the shower stall was running full blast, the shower stall door hanging open. Olivia had jumped out right after her first scream. She was dripping wet, trembling and completely heart-stoppingly naked.

And then he saw why she'd screamed and run out of the stall.

There was a rat in the stall and at first glance, the rodent looked to be just a shade smaller than a miniature pony.

As if aware of his audience, the rat ran out of the stall and scurried over in Olivia's direction. Jumping back, she screamed for a third time.

Wanting to stop the rat before it reached Olivia, Rick looked around for something to hit it with. There was nothing. He did the only thing he could. Taking aim, he shot the rat.

Stifling a scream, Olivia began to sob. She was still trembling. Ordinarily, she would have held together, but the encounter with the rat had been the catalyst, the proverbial final straw. Everything that she had been struggling with to keep under wraps, to keep bottled up inside her just came pouring out.

Confronted by this gut-twisting pain and anguish, Rick did what anyone else would have done. He did what came naturally. Murmuring words meant to soothe, he took Olivia into his arms to reassure her and to offer her comfort.

"It's okay," he said, repeating the two words over and over again like a healing mantra. "It's okay. The rat's dead. He can't get at you anymore." Holding her close to him, acutely aware that only one of them was dressed, he tried not to allow his mind to make the most of that input. Instead, he focused on what had transpired and what needed to be ascertained. "Did he bite you?"

"No."

Rick was afraid she might have gone into shock, but

he couldn't very well begin a detailed exam, searching her body for bite marks. All he could do was press home the point. "Are you sure?"

Shaken, she nodded. "I'm sure."

He felt the words vibrating into his shoulder, accompanied by warm breath that seemed to brand his very skin.

"I'm sorry," Olivia apologized, in between the sobs she was trying to stifle. "I don't usually fall apart like this. It was just a stupid rat. But he climbed right into the stall and his face was inches from mine and I—I—"

She couldn't stop sobbing. Very gently, Rick stroked her hair, telling her over and over again that it was all right, that she'd had a lot to deal with and it wasn't the rat that she was crying about, but everything else.

"But it's going to be all right. I promise."

The words he said got to her. They made her feel defenseless and vulnerable. And yet, at the same time, they made her feel safe, because he understood, understood maybe better than she did what she was going through.

She clung to him, trying to hang on to his strength, trying desperately to get her own back.

And then somehow, somewhere in the middle of the sobs and the soothing words, she lost herself.

Looking back later, Olivia wouldn't be able to say with any certainty just what steps came next and who really was responsible for what.

One moment, she was crying her heart out, damning her poor self-control for breaking down this way. The next moment, she'd turned up her face to his and found herself kissing him.

Or maybe he was kissing her.

Whichever way it started, several seconds into it they were kissing each other. Kissing with a passion and a longing that both surprised and frightened her even as she reveled in the feel of it. Reveled in the wondrous heat that the kiss was generating. It flowed to every part of her starting from the center on out.

She felt alive and vibrant for the first time in years.

Olivia clung to him, digging her fingers into his shoulders as if to reassure herself that he was real, that this was happening. As the kiss grew, deepening, making her feel as if she was sinking inside of it, she became completely disoriented and lost. But it was a good lost. At least for now.

Damn it, what the hell was he doing?

He'd broken down the door and burst into the room to help her, thinking to possibly save her from whatever had made her scream like that. He hadn't come running to the rescue like that simply to have his own turn with her. He had no intention of taking advantage of her.

The woman was naked. And he had seen every single magnificent curve, even as he went to offer her comfort.

Offer her comfort, he silently jeered. He should be giving her something to put on, not draping her on himself as if she were some sort of human shirt.

What the hell was the matter with him? What was he thinking?

That was just the problem, he realized. He wasn't thinking, wasn't thinking at all, just feeling and react-ing. And savoring one of the sweetest kisses, one of the sultriest bodies he had *ever* come across in his thirty-one years on this planet.

Let go of her, damn it. Let go of her.

But he couldn't.

Not when everything inside of him had suddenly gone on tactical alert, responding to the incredible stimuli he had right before him.

He could feel himself losing ground. Giving in by inches. Giving in to the attraction that had been building within him ever since he'd first seen Olivia come striding into Miss Joan's diner, fire in her eyes and all but literally loaded for bear.

There was no excuse for what he was doing. No excuse for savoring her kiss, her nearness. No excuse for holding on to her so tightly, feeling her body heat penetrate his own.

Anger and disappointment struggled for possession of him, trying to wrench the thin strands of control away from the rest of him. The part that didn't have the same moral code as he had been instilled with, obviously.

And he discovered that the longer the kiss went on, the more he wanted to build on the emotion that it kicked up. Build on it and make love with this woman who'd come into his life out of the blue like an unexpected hurricane.

Being with her here in this fleabag of a motel, kissing her and feeling the burn from within only served to remind him just how very empty his life had become.

Chapter Thirteen

Rick honestly had no idea where he ultimately found the inner resolve and strength, but he did and he was able to force himself to pull back before anything happened.

Pausing for a moment to pull himself together, he made sure that he looked only into Olivia's eyes when he spoke to her. If he looked elsewhere, the words just wouldn't come out. The woman's body left him all but completely speechless.

He nodded his head toward the towel rack. "Maybe you should put a towel on."

Had she done something wrong? Why was he backing away?

Embarrassed, horribly uncomfortable, Olivia tried to cover by resorting to a wisecrack. "I would have expected you to ask me to put on high heels, not a towel."

The image of Olivia, her supple body completely nude except for a pair of black stilettos nearly made him swallow his own tongue. He could feel the heat rushing over his body, the almost insurmountable desire to pull her back into his arms and lose himself in her all over again. That he didn't, that he held himself in check, made him superhuman.

"I'm sorry," she began, quickly reaching for the lone towel that hung on the rack.

But as she pulled the towel to her, the rack, barely attached to the wall by badly rusted screws, came flying away and fell to the floor. It landed within a hairbreadth from her foot, and would have hit her if she hadn't jumped. But that threw her off balance and she wound up bumping up against Rick.

Instincts had him closing his arms around her to keep Olivia upright.

And then they were back to square one, with his hormones raging, begging for release. The scent in her hair filled his head, further lowering his resistance. "You know, there's only so many times that I can pull away," he told her.

Olivia turned around in the circle of his arms, facing him, her body tingling. Eager. She had to know. "Why do you want to pull away?"

"Want to?" he echoed incredulously. "Is that what you think? I *don't* want to," he assured her. "I'm doing it for you. I don't want you making a mistake."

Her heart all but melted right there in her chest. "Maybe I don't think it is a mistake." She searched his face, trying to read what was on his mind. But she couldn't. She could only hope. "Do you?"

His eyes held hers. "I don't know what to think," he said honestly.

"Then maybe you and I shouldn't think at all. Maybe," she continued, raising herself up on her toes, her lips achingly close to his, "we should just let things happen and see where it goes."

Straight to hell on a toboggan, Rick couldn't help thinking. But he couldn't very well tell himself that he was being noble and shielding Olivia if she didn't want to be shielded. And heaven knew he was hungry, as hungry as a man coming off a forty-day fast.

He couldn't remember the last time he'd been with a woman. The last time being with a woman had mattered to him, he'd been with Alycia. The night before she'd died in the crash.

Although he didn't want it to, Rick had the feeling this time would matter. Making love with this woman would leave a lasting impression on him. It would change him.

But it was far too late to put on the brakes, too late to walk away. Because she'd turned her face up to his, offering him something he wanted more than anything else in the world.

He wanted her.

As gently as if she was in danger of shattering, Rick took her into his arms and drew her to him. He softly touched his lips to hers. The sweetness of her kiss took his breath away and his heart began to hammer wildly.

As did hers.

He could feel the way it beat against his chest. Could feel her heartbeat echoing within him until two hearts had somehow melded into a single one.

He wasn't quite sure when the frenzy took hold, but the tempo of the inner music between them increased and the gentle kiss deepened until there was nothing gentle about it.

He kissed her over and over again, finding that the more he kissed her, the more he wanted to. She put a fire in his belly the likes of which he hadn't experienced in a long, long time.

All of her life, she had measured twice before cutting once. She had always been so cautious, so careful that she'd earned the teasing nickname of "Grandmother Olivia" when she was just in junior high school. The nickname followed her all the way to college.

She didn't care, because reckless actions had consequences and would have gotten in the way of her making something of herself. And even if she were given to reckless behavior, she didn't have that luxury, because there wasn't just herself to think of. There was Tina, always Tina. Even if she had wanted to be wild, she couldn't take the risk because she always had to be there for Tina.

But being there for Tina hadn't exactly worked out all that well, had it? All those years of behaving, of being restrained, of thinking everything through to its conclusion not once but several times, that all seemed wasted now. Tina had rebelled and not only gotten pregnant, but then run off with the father of her baby, leaving her to rattle around alone in her expensive, empty high-rise apartment.

With all that in her background, Olivia saw no reason not to give in to this incredible pull, the overwhelming attraction to this man that surged in her veins.

Her mouth sealed to his, Olivia fumbled with the buttons on his shirt, working them through the holes until the material hung freely about his torso. She eagerly yanked the shirt from his shoulders, from his body, wanting to touch him.

Olivia ran her palms over his hard torso, gliding her fingers over the ridges of his abdominal muscles the way she'd longed to do ever since she'd seen Rick walk into his kitchen with his shirt hanging open.

The hardness she discovered sent a jolting electric current zipping through her veins, at the same time that it moistened her very core.

She wanted him, wanted him to make love with her, to kiss her until she was mindless. Their lips locked in a kiss, they somehow managed to stumble their way out of the bathroom, working their way into the bedroom. The path was marked with clothing that had been shed.

With each new frontier she crossed—taking off his shirt, his jeans, sliding her hands along his underwear and tugging at it, teasing herself as well as him—her breathing grew progressively labored. Maintaining focus became difficult. Her mind was spiraling out of control.

She bit her lower lip to keep from crying out as he trailed his lips along the side of her neck, nibbling at her sensitized skin. He set off fireworks within her. Showers of blues, reds, golds, greens and so many more exquisite, indescribable colors danced through her mind's eye as Rick lowered her to the bed.

She felt as weak as a thin thread and as resiliently strong as a steel wire as Rick brushed his lips along the more sensitive areas of her body, bringing about a quickening that was equal to nothing she'd ever experienced before.

As he explored, caressed, suckled, the excitement within her grew until she almost couldn't breathe, couldn't pull in enough air to sustain herself. A cry of ecstasy escaped as she felt his tongue taking possession of her, inciting a mini-riot within her very core.

She gasped, bucking, arching, trying to follow the feeling, to frame it and hang on in order to prolong the climax.

When it was done, when she couldn't hold on to even a sliver of it a second longer, Olivia fell back on the bed, exhausted and all but disoriented. In a haze, she thought she heard Rick laugh softly and then felt the warmth beginning all over again as he started to take her on a second journey, the route different, the result identical.

This time, she cried out his name, clutching at his shoulders like a woman about to go spinning off the edge of the earth and desperately trying to anchor herself before that happened.

Before she disappeared into space and became nothing more than a speck in the heavens.

And then, suddenly, he was there, just above her, distributing his weight equally between his arms, his hands firmly planted on the mattress on either side of her.

A heartbeat earlier, she'd felt the hard contours of his body as he'd pulled himself up along hers. The quickening within her core began just on the promise of what was to come. She was more than ready for him, more than ready to share the moment rather than to experience its wonders alone, the way she'd just been doing thanks to his clever actions.

Or she *thought* she was ready for him.

There was no way she could have been prepared for this. For the crackling rhythm that flashed through her body over and over again as he entered her and then began to move his hips. She breathlessly hurried to synchronize her movements to his.

They went faster and faster, racing to catch the ride of their lives.

She heard him make a sound as he was swept up in the moment and heard her own voice blending with his as the whirlpool seized them both at the same time, lifting them up, freezing in the moment and then, slowly, receding again.

She couldn't catch her breath. And quite possibly, she would *never* catch her breath again. But it had been worth it because this, she knew, was going to be the one precious experience of a lifetime.

Her lifetime.

Oh, she'd made love before, if she could actually apply the label to that. Couplings would be a more adequate description. A handful of couplings that had turned out to be far less than memorable events. The experiences had been so forgettable that she would have been hard-pressed to recall the faces of any of the men who had shared, however briefly, a bed with her. At that time, to her, sex had become much ado about nothing.

But this, she knew, would be something she would always remember—vividly—even when she blew out a hundred candles on her birthday cake. Time would never dim the memory of this.

Olivia felt him withdraw, felt the mattress—rather than the earth—move as Rick fell back beside her. She waited for him to get up, to gather together his clothes and get dressed, behaving, more or less, as if nothing had happened.

Or, if not that, then she expected him to roll over and go to sleep, exhausted by the pinnacles they had both just climbed.

What she *didn't* expect him to do was what he did.

She didn't expect him to slip his arm around her and pull her close to him. Nor did she expect him to press a kiss to her temple as he released a sigh that sounded as if its source went down deeper than even his soul. After having her entire world rocked, she did not expect tenderness on top of that.

Yet that was exactly what she got.

"You are one incredible lady," he murmured against her temple. The words made her even warmer than his breath did as it danced along her skin all the way down to her neck.

"Me?"

In her estimation, she'd done nothing to merit his words. He was an incredible lover. A man who'd played her body as if it was a rare, finely tuned, precious violin. Yes, she'd responded to him but the comparison between the two of them couldn't be measured by any kind of instrument known to man.

Olivia turned in to him, expecting to see a smile of amusement on his lips.

He was smiling all right, but she could see that he was also serious. How was that possible? He was the one who'd made the earth not only move, but explode. It was all his doing, not hers. He had to know that.

"You," he confirmed. As he spoke, he toyed with a

strand of her hair, winding and unwinding it around his finger. Anticipation began to move through her. "I guess it's true what they say."

"What who says?"

"They," he repeated with a smile. "The all-important 'they.'"

"And what is it that they say?" she asked, still not following him but content to remain like this, lying here with him, feeling the heat of his body as it reached out to hers. This was the perfect moment. If she were to die now, this minute, she would die utterly content.

"That still waters run deep."

She thought of the past half hour, steeped in mounting frenzy. There'd been perpetual motion involved. "I wasn't aware that I was so *still*."

"Well, not strictly speaking," he admitted, a widening smile curving the corners of his mouth and going straight to her heart. "But talking to you someone might get the impression that you took yourself too seriously to let go like that." He tucked her against his side and before she could say anything about his evaluation, he added, "You took my breath away."

Any protest she might have had to offer died instantly. Another reaction rose in its place. Affection swirled through her and, while she knew it had no future and that she couldn't allow herself to get too caught up in this feeling, for the moment, for right here, right now, she gave herself permission to savor it. To revel in it. And to pretend, just for an instant, that it would last.

Olivia cupped her palm along his cheek, feeling things that had never had a place in her life before. "The feeling, Sheriff Santiago," she said, enunciating his title and name slowly, seductively, "is more than mutual." She teasingly brushed his lips with her own. "What's that expression?" It was a rhetorical question, she was well aware of the expression she was about to use. "Ridden hard and put away wet? That's just how I feel."

He did his best to look serious. "Is that a complaint?"

She laughed softly. "That is so far from a complaint, Sheriff, that it's not even remotely in the same time zone."

Humor glinted in his eyes. "So you wouldn't mind, if say, you and I went out for another ride?"

"You want to do it again?" she asked, staring at him, stunned. She would have thought that after a performance like that, he was done for the night.

Obviously she knew nothing about this man.

He grinned at her and she realized that she really liked his grin. "Nothing much else to do," he answered philosophically. "It's raining outside and the TV's down."

Another delighted laugh broke through. "You do know how to sweet-talk a girl, Sheriff."

"No, not a girl," he contradicted, lightly kissing the side of her neck. "A woman. Because you, lady, are *all* woman."

There went her heart again, she thought, pounding wildly and wickedly. "You really do know how to turn a phrase," she breathed as the fireworks inside of her began all over again.

It was the last thing she said to him for quite some time.

Chapter Fourteen

"I am very sorry to hear about your sister, Olivia, but you have a responsibility to the firm that cannot be suspended at will," the cold, scratchy tenor voice on the other end of the line informed her. "I am sure that you've considered the fact that your sister may never wake up from her coma. One way or the other, there will be staggering bills to pay. Your erstwhile dedication to her won't pay for a single IV. However, your position here at the firm will. Surely you can see that you have a moral obligation to return to us immediately."

Olivia sat on the bed in what had temporarily become her room, listening to the senior-senior partner, Harris Norvil, lecturing her. Mentally, she caught herself throwing up defenses and doing her best to block out the gray-haired man's words.

It was Friday morning, two days after she and Rick had sought shelter from the storm and discovered it in each other's arms. It'd been a full week since she'd arrived in Forever and she now realized that she would need to stay longer.

Wanting to give the firm a heads-up sooner than later, she'd called to request an extension for her leave of absence. That way, they could find someone to handle her cases. Initially, she expected to speak to the head administrative assistant, but the moment she identified herself to the woman, she was asked to please hold. The next voice she heard was the cold, sharp voice of Harris Norvil. He wielded guilt like a finely honed saber, slicing the air with every word he spoke.

This was not going to be easy. "I'm afraid I can't return immediately, Mr. Norvil."

She could almost see the man pulling back his bony shoulders beneath his hand-tailored suit, a dour expression on his face. His gray eyes narrowing into slits.

"Can't or won't?"

"Can't," she replied, trying very hard to maintain a respectful tone and not allow her temper to break through.

The man lived and breathed the firm, she understood that, but the firm did not define who and what she was any longer. She'd had a rude awakening this past week and realized what was really important. Burning the midnight oil at Norvil and Tyler was not it. She had a life outside the briefs and the long, drawn-out court procedures.

Even before this had come up, she had begun feeling disillusioned with the whole process. It occurred to her that victory in the courtroom wasn't about justice; it was about who was the most clever at blocking motions, trumping testimonies and manipulating the facts to their own best advantage. That left a bad taste in her mouth.

"My car broke down when I arrived in Forever," she

explained, "and the mechanic had to send out for parts. I'm told they're arriving today, possibly tomorrow."

She could tell by the way he breathed heavily that Norvil did not find the excuse satisfactory. "Take a plane."

"I'm afraid that there is no airport in the vicinity."

She heard Norvil mutter an oath. He made no effort to keep it inaudible. "Rent a car and drive back."

"There are no car rentals around here, either."

Norvil lost his temper. "Where the hell are you, Dogpatch?"

Ordinarily, the senior partner losing his temper would have made her retrace her steps and tread lightly, but she felt oddly combative, and also protective of the town that she herself had looked down upon only a few days earlier. What a difference a couple of days made.

"Not every town is as urban as Dallas, but Forever has its charm."

The people here were good people. They went out of their way to help one another out. And they'd been good to her. She and Tina had lived in the high-rise apartment for three years now and she still didn't even know her neighbors' names, much less feel comfortable enough to trust that neighbor with Bobby for a few hours. Yet she had absolutely no qualms about leaving the infant with Miss Joan or Lupe.

"All right," Norvil snapped, "we'll send a car for you."

He could send a coach made out of a pumpkin, drawn by four horses that had once been mice and she wasn't leaving, not without Tina.

"I'm sorry, sir," Olivia said firmly, "but I have to

respectfully decline your generous offer. I have to stay here until my sister can be transferred to another hospital."

There was silence on the other end of the line and she braced herself for an eruption. Norvil's were known to be legendary once they got underway. But when he finally spoke again, Norvil's voice was colder than ever, and exceedingly precise.

"All right, Ms. Blayne, one more week. But that's it. If you choose to remain there longer than that, we will be forced to terminate you and send your things to your apartment. Do I make myself clear?"

He was threatening her. And, for the sake of having a career to go back to at the end of this whole thing, she would let him get away with it. Worse, she would act grateful. God, but she hated this.

"Yes, sir, perfectly clear. That's very generous of you, Mr. Norvil. Thank you."

But she was talking to a dead line. Norvil had hung up. Muttering a curse, Olivia snapped her cell phone shut.

"Problem?"

She looked up to see Rick standing in the doorway. How much had he heard, she wondered. She hadn't thought to close the door. Things had gotten a great deal more relaxed between them since their return from the motel room. The magical night they'd spent together had stretched beyond its parameters, spilling out into the subsequent evenings that followed. She'd never known that being stranded could be so wonderful.

She blew out a long breath. "Not unless you call groveling a problem." She rose from the bed. "I just asked the senior partner at my firm for an extension on my emergency leave of absence. He made it sound as if I was asking for his last pint of blood."

Olivia forced a smile to her lips, refusing to fixate on the fact that she had, more than likely, torpedoed her chances of getting a raise this year. Norvil not only demanded team players—which was his right—but that those players live and breathe the firm to the exclusion of everything else—which *wasn't* his right.

Her eyes met Rick's. "Which isn't possible. Everyone knows the man runs on pure motor oil."

He came closer to her and touched her shoulder. She was hard-pressed to remember ever feeling anything more intimate, at least with her clothes on.

"You okay?" he asked.

A defiant smile rose to her lips as she tossed her head. "I am terrific."

He grinned in response. "You'll get no argument from me. So, are you ready to go?" he asked, crossing over to where Bobby lay in the playpen.

Rather than waiting for Olivia to make the first move, he picked up the baby and then grabbed hold of the diaper bag that was literally stuffed with everything that the infant would need for the day.

Rick appeared so comfortable doing that, she thought, feeling a familiar warmth stir within her. When had this happened? When had she started longing for what she'd always turned her back on? A husband, a child. A family of her own.

Tina had always been enough family for her. At times, maybe even too much family. And now, suddenly, she was thinking picket fences and all that went with them. What was going on with her?

Had to be something in the water. Or maybe with the town. When she'd arrived, the various citizens of Forever had been busy decorating for Christmas. Now, she thought, it was like wandering onto the set of *It's A Wonderful Life,* except that this was real.

Turning around with Bobby in his arms, Rick paused. "What are you thinking?"

The corners of her mouth curved just a little. "That maybe I'm the one who's in a coma and that this is all a dream."

"You certainly didn't act like someone in a coma last night," Rick pointed out with a grin.

Last night had been another magical night, except that there were no rats-on-steroids to drive her into his arms. It had taken just a look, the promise of a kiss, and she was there. Knowing full well their relationship was finite, she allowed herself to let down her defenses and *really* enjoy herself.

She wasn't quite sure how to respond to what he'd just said. When it came to legal matters, she had everything at her fingertips and there was no hesitation in her comebacks. But a lover's compliment put her in uncharted territory. She had no idea what to say or do, other than to savor it.

Before she could even attempt to form any sort of a response, her phone rang. Olivia didn't bother suppressing a sigh.

"Probably Norvil, calling to rescind the extension," she guessed. Pressing the talk button on the cell, she said, "Blayne."

"Miss Blayne? It's Dr. Baker."

The instant she heard the physician's voice, her hand tightened on the small cell, almost snapping it in half. Was he calling to tell her that Tina had slipped away in the night?

Tension rendered her whole body utterly rigid. She barely had enough oxygen in her lungs to be able to speak. "Yes, Doctor?"

Rick had been about to step out of the room to give her privacy, but he saw her grow pale and knew that his place was here, to help any way he could. When he heard Olivia say "doctor" he became alert, nearly as tense as she was.

"She's awake," Baker said without any preamble.

Olivia went numb.

Had she imagined what he'd just said? At this point, it was too wonderful to contemplate. Her breath was all but gone as she asked, "What?"

"Your sister's awake," the jovial voice on the other end declared. "I thought you might want to know in case you were planning to skip coming today."

"Not a chance," Olivia cried happily, tears filling her eyes. "Thank you. Thank you for calling. Thank you for being there for her," she added. She bit her lower lip to keep from babbling.

She'd gone to the hospital every day and every day, the doctor had made a point of coming in to give her an update of the hours since she'd been there last. He told her of any progress that had taken place, or any changes—both good and bad—that had been noted in the nurses' files.

"Just doing my job," he told her without any fanfare.

"I'll be by to look in on her later," he promised just before he hung up.

"Good news?" Rick surmised as she closed her cell phone. She gave him her answer by throwing her arms around him and the baby. Bobby squealed. "I think you're crowding him." Rick laughed. "So, what did the doctor say?"

"That Tina's awake. That she's finally awake." Olivia's voice cracked. She steepled her fingers before her lips, afraid of bursting into sobs. "She's going to be all right, Rick. Tina's really going to be all right."

He looked at her solemnly and merely nodded. And then a smile peeked through as he said, "Told you so."

"Go ahead and gloat." She laughed, blinking back tears. "I'm too happy to care. Besides, you earned the right. You told me not to give up—and you were right."

"I'm the sheriff," he reminded her. "I'm supposed to be right. It's in the town's bylaws." He glanced at the baby in his arms. "Do you want to take the baby with you to the hospital instead of dropping him of with Miss Joan?" he asked. She looked at him quizzically. "It might do your sister some good to see her son looking so well, especially if you decide to tell her about her boyfriend."

She should have thought of that, Olivia upbraided herself. Rick shouldn't have to be the voice of reason.

Her head was swimming, and it was hard for her to grab on to a coherent thought. She smiled at him, feeling incredibly close to this man she knew so little about.

"I'm glad you're here," she told him.

He told himself not to take the remark to heart. She

was just reacting to the situation and didn't mean what she said. Soon, she'd be leaving and it wasn't a good idea to allow himself to become too attached.

"Just doing my job."

That was the second time she'd heard that in the past five minutes. No one in these small towns thought they were doing anything out of the ordinary, going out of their ways for someone else. Collectively, these people were just the best people she'd ever encountered.

"C'mon," Rick told her, pressing a kiss to her forehead, "we'd better hit the road. If she's up to it, you and your sister have a lot of catching up to do. But you have to tell me one thing," he said as he ushered her out of the room, one arm cradling her nephew, the other pressed to the small of her back.

"Sure," she agreed freely, an act that took her completely by surprise and that she found oddly liberating, "if I can."

"If you're so happy—and you should be—why are you crying? Because you shouldn't be," he said. He had never been able to understand why women cried if they weren't upset or devastatingly unhappy.

Olivia couldn't explain the logistics, she just knew she was happy enough to burst, not to mention relieved. For some reason, this brought moisture to her eyes. She shrugged helplessly as she felt another wave of tears forming.

"Just happiness spilling out, I guess," she told him.

He shook his head as the three of them left the house. He didn't bother locking the door behind him. Her explanation hadn't really shed any light on the situation. "If you say so."

THOUGH NO TRAFFIC impeded the way, getting to the hospital seemed to take twice as long this time. Toward the end, Olivia grappled with the very real urge to jump out of the vehicle and run the rest of the way. The same feeling she'd had the first day Rick had driven her here.

She leaped out of the car before he'd barely pulled into a parking space. It was Rick who grounded her, who acted like the voice of reason. By example, he forced her to calm down and behave rationally, or at least with some semblance of rationality.

They entered the hospital together, although Olivia led the way by some several steps. When they reached the ICU, Rick hung back.

"Why don't I stay out here with Bobby and you go in first?" Rick suggested. "Spend a little time with her and see how well she's doing and what you think she might feel up to?"

Olivia nodded. Again, he was the calm in the middle of the storm. She should be the one thinking logically instead of acting so scattered.

Now that she stood outside her sister's room, she was almost afraid to enter. Afraid that Tina had slipped back into her coma, or that she'd sustained brain damage during the accident and was no longer the Tina she knew. She hadn't thought of that until just now and the prospect of it put fear into her heart.

Taking a deep breath, she slowly opened the door and walked into Tina's room.

Tina's eyes were closed. Olivia pressed her lips together, fearing the worst, that there had been a window of opportunity to catch her sister awake and she'd missed it. She hadn't gotten here fast enough.

She'd known someone whose cousin had come out of his coma for a full half hour before slipping back and dying the same day. She couldn't bear that. She just couldn't.

Starting to pray, she tiptoed over to her sister's bed and took hold of Tina's hand. "Please wake up, Tina," she begged in a fervent whisper. "Please wake up."

"Just five more minutes, Livy," Tina murmured. Her eyes were still shut.

Olivia suppressed a cry, tried to tamp down a sudden surge of joy. Tina always used to beg for more time each morning when she tried to get her up for school.

And then Tina opened her eyes, a very weak smile on her lips. It took her a second filled with disbelief to realize what was happening. Tina was playing a joke on her. It meant that Tina's mental faculties were working. No brain damage.

Thank you, God. I owe you. Big time.

"No, you get out of bed right now, Christina," Olivia said, trying to remember exactly what she used to say every morning as she bullied her sister out of bed. "School's not going to come to you, you have to go to it." And then she gave up the ruse, unable to continue. She blinked back tears. "Welcome back, kid. You gave me quite a scare."

Tina smiled weakly at her. "You came for me, Livy. I knew you would. I knew you would," she repeated, her voice growing reedy. And then her eyes filled with tears. "I'm sorry about the car."

Olivia shook her head. "Cars can be replaced, Tina."

She touched her sister's cheek. It felt cooler than she was happy about. "You can't. And you're still here," she added, giving her hand a small squeeze. "Everything's going to be all right," she promised.

Events began to come back to Tina. Memories unfurled like flags in the wind. Her last waking hours flashed through her mind.

Her eyes widened in horror.

"Bobby." Her fingers dug into her sister's wrist in alarm. "Oh God, Livy, I had to leave him on this cop's doorstep. Don said he wanted us all to die together. He was talking crazy, but I managed to convince him to let me leave the baby behind. I didn't have much time. And now I can't remember where—"

"Tina, I have him. I have him," Olivia cried, breaking into her sister's sob. "Bobby's safe."

"Thank you." Tina closed her eyes, relieved. "Thank you," she repeated. Tears seeped through her lashes onto her cheeks and then slid down until they reached all the way down her neck. "You always could manage things so much better than me."

"That'll change," Olivia promised her. "When you're better."

Tina opened her eyes again. "I only wish," she murmured softly.

"Look at me, Tina," Olivia ordered. "You *are* going to get better."

"But nothing's going to change," Tina cried sadly. "Don'll never let me go."

"Don's not a threat to you any longer," Olivia told her.

Tina shook her head, refusing to be comforted.

"You don't know him like I do, Livy. Don won't stop until he—"

"Tina, sweetheart." She took her sister's hand between hers. "He can't hurt you anymore. He can't hurt either one of you anymore," Olivia told her. "Tina, Don's dead."

Chapter Fifteen

For a moment, it was so quiet in Tina's room that all Olivia could hear were the machines as they monitored her sister's vital signs. Maybe she shouldn't have said anything yet. Tina seemed blindsided by the news. She was about to call for a nurse when Tina finally spoke.

"He's dead?" the younger woman asked in a small, still voice that was devoid of any emotion, any indication of what, if anything, she was feeling.

Olivia braced herself. For what, she didn't know. "Yes."

Tina's eyes held hers. Tina's were filled with disbelief and confusion. "You're sure?"

"Yes." Olivia thought she perceived an inkling of relief in her sister's voice. "Morgue, toe-tag, autopsy sure." What she would have wanted to add was "good riddance," but Tina had been in love with the monster, at least at one point, so she did her best to sound neutral. Most of all, she wanted to be supportive of her sister. "I'm sorry, Tina, but he is gone. The doctor told me that Don died immediately when the car struck the utility pole."

Tina's blue eyes shimmered as they filled with tears.

"That was what he wanted." She raised her chin ever so slightly, an unconscious sign of triumph that she had managed to survive. "Except that he wanted the baby and me to die with him."

How dare he? Olivia's hands clenched into fists. She struggled not to let her temper flare and rail at the man who was no longer there. "Yeah, well, I'm very, very glad it didn't happen that way." She heard the door opening and knew without turning around who had come in. Rick was bringing the baby in for Tina.

The man was good, she thought. He'd even had the timing for his entrance right.

"And so is someone else," she told Tina.

Turning, Olivia held out her arms and Rick passed Bobby to her. Though most doctors would argue against it, she was certain that Bobby recognized his mother. A contented sound escaped the small, rosebudlike mouth.

"Oh Bobby, Bobby, you're all right," Tina sobbed. She pressed the control attached to her bed until she was almost in a sitting position.

Olivia moved around so that Tina was able to see her infant son more easily.

"I think you're probably too weak to hold him, Tina, but I can hold him against you," Olivia offered, extending her arms so that Bobby could nuzzle against his mother.

Tina closed her eyes for a moment as she breathed in the very sweet, powdery smell that all babies had in common. When she opened her eyes, she looked at Olivia with gratitude. "This is all I need to get well, just to see my baby. I'm going to do better, Livy. I swear I'm going to do better."

Olivia smiled. "I have no doubts," she answered Tina with feeling.

For the first time since he'd entered, Tina became aware of the other person in the room.

"This is Sheriff Enrique Santiago, the man whose doorstep you left Bobby on," Olivia explained.

"Are you here to arrest me?" Tina asked hesitantly.

"No, ma'am, I'm here to see you reunited with your son," he told her. "Leaving him was clearly an act of desperation. You did it to save him. It's what mothers do," he assured her gently.

Not his mother, of course, he couldn't help thinking, but at least she'd had the presence of mind to leave his sister and him with her mother-in-law rather than skipping out on them entirely, leaving them in an empty apartment to fend for themselves.

OLIVIA AND BOBBY, with Rick keeping to the background, remained with Tina as long as they could. When she began showing signs of growing tired, they left, promising to return the next day.

Before leaving, Olivia stopped at the central desk and had her sister's attending physician paged.

Baker saw her standing in the hallway with the sheriff as he came around the corner from the emergency room. "I take it you saw her," the physician said. The smile on the man's somewhat craggy face was a combination of satisfaction and warmth.

She hadn't thought he had it in him to actually help Tina, but she was wrong. Olivia was more than willing—and happy—to give the surgeon his due. "I can't tell you how relieved I am to see my sister finally open her eyes again."

Baker laughed, nodding. His features softened. "You're not the only one. I've been at this doctoring gig a long time, but I still get a rush with each patient's recovery," he confessed.

His honesty surprised her. The doctors she knew were excellent, but for the most part, removed. There always seemed to be an invisible barrier between doctor and patient. Maybe it wasn't so bad in these small towns after all. "When do you think that she'll be up to being transferred?"

The surgeon thought for a moment before answering. "Tina needs to stay here a few more days," Baker told her. "Then, if everything continues on this path, she can go home."

He didn't actually mean home, did he? "To the hospital." It was half a question on her part.

Baker's smile widened as his glance took them both in. "Not unless she lives in one," he told her.

Olivia stared at him, afraid to believe what she thought he was saying. "You mean she can go home-home?" She heard Rick suppress a laugh behind her but she didn't turn around. She waited for the doctor's answer.

"Yes. Home-home," he said, echoing her phrase. "Tina'll need follow-up care, of course. For that she can see her own physician or, if you like," he continued, taking a prescription pad out of his pocket, "I can refer you to someone." He began writing the man's name and phone number. "Dr. Mike Delaney, he practices out in your area." Finished writing, he tore off the four-by-six sheet and handed it to her. "We interned together at Johns Hopkins in Baltimore. He's excellent."

Johns Hopkins was one of the best hospitals in the country, she thought. They didn't turn out mediocre doctors. The physicians who graduated from there were top-notch. And yet, Baker was here. It didn't make any sense to her. Very slowly, she folded the paper with one hand and slipped it into her purse.

"If you don't mind my asking, Dr. Baker—if you were good enough to attend Johns Hopkins, what are you doing here?"

The look on his face told her that this wasn't the first time he'd been asked the question. But there was no irritation in his voice as he said, "Because small towns need good doctors, too. Besides, Pine Ridge is my hometown. It feels good to give back a little something." His tone told her the subject was officially closed. "Now, your sister's doing fine. She has a remarkable constitution so, despite my being guardedly optimistic, I can honestly tell you that she's coming along like gangbusters."

She wanted to believe that, but she had always been the cautious type. It was better to be braced than devastated. "But she was in that coma for so long."

"Sometimes, the body knows best. Being in a coma allowed her body to focus exclusively on healing her wounds. And it obviously worked," he pronounced, pleased. Baker fished a card out of his other pocket and handed that to her as well. "If you think of any other questions, call me."

She looked down at the card in her hand, focusing on the phone number printed in black against the stark white background. "Is that the number of your service?"

"No," Baker told her, "that's the number to my cell. I find the personal touch works better in Pine Ridge. And it works better for me, too," he added.

She thanked him again with feeling, thinking how lucky Tina was that this man decided to "give something back" to the town where he'd been born. And then she, Rick and the baby left the hospital to go home.

She thought how good that phrase sounded, and then pushed back the thought and the feeling that the phrase generated before she started to get carried away. She knew the feeling had nowhere to go.

"Thank you for staying—at the hospital," she clarified when Rick glanced in her direction. For most of the trip home, she'd been quiet, pensive. He did his part and had left her alone. The radio droned on inaudibly in the background. "I was afraid you might leave, as usual." It just seemed right, having him there with her when she spoke to Tina.

"Special occasion." He then added in a neutral tone, "Seemed like the right thing to do."

He was constantly downplaying his actions. Didn't he know how unique he was? How good? "You've been really wonderful about all this. I don't know where to begin to thank you."

"You just did," he told her. Being on the receiving end of gratitude embarrassed him. He rolled her words over in his head a second time. "Actually, that sounded pretty final. You're not thinking of leaving just yet, are you?"

She shook her head. "I can't without Tina. I *was* going to have her transferred to a hospital in Dallas, but she really does seem to be getting excellent care here and the last thing I want to do is risk upsetting her progress. That means I'll stay in Forever until Dr. Baker releases Tina. I guess you're still stuck with me." It suddenly occurred to her that although she found the nights wonderful, Rick might feel he hadn't signed on for this length of time. Her eyes shifted to him. "Unless—"

He could see where this was going. Olivia was a beautiful, sharp woman, but not nearly as confident as she wanted the world to believe. Beneath the expensive suits and the aristocratic, classy lines was a small, somewhat insecure young girl who had never had the chance to lean on anyone for support. He found himself wanting to be the one whose shoulder she sought out.

"I wouldn't exactly call it 'stuck,' Livy," he told her.

She desperately wanted to ask him what he would call it, but was afraid of pushing her luck. This little gem he'd just dropped would have to be enough.

"Oh," she said.

"Besides," he continued, "I was thinking of putting you to work tonight."

"Oh?" This time, the single word was far more alert and cautious.

He nodded as he watched his high beams cut through the darkness on the road. "I've got a box of Christmas decorations that I've been meaning to put up. My sister's planning on coming home Christmas Day. She claims that the house looks happier when it's decorated for Christmas. So, if you don't mind joining me…"

Last year, she'd been too busy to do Christmas, and Tina was out of the house more than she was in, so there didn't seem to be a point. She hadn't even put up a tree—not even the small artificial kind. The upshot was that she felt as if Christmas had bypassed her.

Which meant she was clearly overdue.

The corners of her mouth curved deeply. "I don't mind," she assured him.

"Good."

The sight of his grin warmed her the rest of the way back to Forever.

INSTEAD OF GOING straight to his house, Rick surprised her by pulling up at the diner first.

Olivia eyed him quizzically.

"I thought since Miss Joan has been taking care of Bobby, she deserves an update about Bobby's mother."

She should have thought of that, Olivia berated herself. "Sure," she agreed cheerfully.

Rick stepped back, allowing her to enter first.

It was only when she was inside the diner that Olivia realized he had let her go in first on purpose rather than just being polite.

Miss Joan, Lupe, Rick's deputies, Mick the mechanic and several people she had come to know in town were inside the diner and they all shouted "Surprise!" the minute she walked in.

Dumbfounded, Olivia looked from the face of one person to the next, people who had been virtual strangers to her less than two weeks ago.

"What is this?" she asked Miss Joan.

Miss Joan came around the counter to stand beside her. As if she'd been doing it since he was born, she took Bobby into her arms.

"It's your party, honey. We're celebrating your good news—your sister coming out of her coma," the older woman explained in case the theme of the celebration still eluded her.

Olivia found herself without words again. Not a good thing for a trial lawyer, but what she couldn't find in words she more than made up for in feelings. Everything inside of her felt warmed as she basked in the thoughtfulness of these people who had seen fit to cross her path.

She enjoyed herself a great deal.

"How did they find out?" Olivia asked Rick as, hours later, she stood up on tiptoe on the stepladder he'd provided to hang yet another ornament on the tree in his living room.

The tree was fragrant and the scent of pine was everywhere, nudging memories of Christmases gone by from the depths of her mind. She couldn't stop smiling.

"I called to tell them," Rick answered matter-of-factly as he attached a particularly delicate looking angel to a high branch.

But he'd been with her at the hospital the entire time, she thought. "When?"

Rick attached another ornament. "When I was in the hall with Bobby, giving you a few minutes alone with Tina."

Olivia climbed down to retrieve more ornaments. "You are sneaky, Sheriff."

"I prefer the word *clever* myself," he said with a grin.

Noting where she stood, Rick stopped what he was doing, caught her eye and pointed up toward the ceiling.

When she looked, Olivia saw that he had somehow managed to put up a mistletoe without her realizing it. The sheriff of Forever was just chock-full of surprises, she thought warmly.

"More of your cleverness?" she asked as he came closer.

"Absolutely," Rick said, enfolding her into his arms. "One of my better moments, actually."

She could already taste his lips on hers. "You'll get no argument from me."

His grin grew wider. "I really wasn't counting on one," Rick said just before he brought his mouth down on hers.

Olivia sighed with contentment, even as the passion began to build almost instantly, made that much more fierce because she knew her supply of moments like this was limited.

Tina was conscious, meaning she was getting better, and they would be on their way soon, back to Dallas. Back to the ninety-mile-an-hour life that she'd led.

And things would go back to normal for Rick as well. Without her.

Olivia wondered if, in a year's time, he would even remember her name or who she was.

The thought brought an ache into her heart. It wasn't supposed to be there. She'd told herself that she'd accepted these terms the first time she'd made love with

Rick. She'd known that this didn't have the earmarks of "forever" about it. She lived in Dallas and he lived in "Dogpatch," or at least a reasonable facsimile thereof. *And never the twain shall meet.*

Except that it had and he, as the saying went, had rocked her world. Rocked it each and every time they made love. She would never be the same.

"What do you say we finish working on the tree tomorrow?" Rick suggested. The wicked twinkle in his eye utterly fascinated her. Everything about the man fascinated her. She was hopeless. But she might as well enjoy what she had while she had it. Before it faded away.

She was more than willing to go along with his suggestion and nodded. "I always did like the minimalist look," she told him. She did her best to appear serious as she asked, "What do you have in mind?"

Rick surprised her by scooping her into his arms. "Guess."

Olivia laughed, lacing her arms around his neck. Glorying in the feel of his arms around her.

"You'd better do it fast," she coaxed. "Bobby's been asleep for a couple of hours already. He's due to wake up soon."

"Fast it is," Rick said agreeably, brushing his lips against hers just to tease her. "And then, if we have any more time, how do you feel about slow?"

He was kissing the side of her neck in between words, sending her body temperature soaring along with her pulse. Clouding her mind.

"Slow?"

"Uh-huh. Bone-melting, body-achingly slow," he elaborated.

His breath was hot along her skin and her core quickened. It was becoming a familiar response to him, to his very touch. What she was feeling was as close to yearning as she figured she had ever come.

Or ever would.

Her sigh came out ragged as anticipation raced rampantly all through her.

"Slow sounds wonderful. Maybe you should do that first," she managed to get out, each word emerging in slow motion, in direct contrast to the way her heart pounded.

"I am nothing if not a servant of the people," he told her dutifully, the words dancing along her breath-warmed flesh. "Your wish is my command."

"I'll remember that," she breathed with effort. "And I intend to hold you to it."

His eyes were already making love to her face, promising her things that had her whole body tingling with anticipation and excitement.

"See that you do," he deadpanned.

They'd reached his bedroom. Shifting, Rick closed the door with his elbow and then set her down on the comforter as gently as a snowflake.

Olivia held out her arms to him. "Shut up and kiss me."

"More good commands," Rick acknowledged with an approving nod of his head. He slid in next to her to obey this order first.

The kiss was passionate and only built from there.
Bobby did his part by sleeping for another full hour.
The hour didn't go to waste.

Chapter Sixteen

After much waiting for delinquent parts that seemed to take their own sweet time arriving from a dealer close to a hundred miles away, Mick announced with a bit of pleased fanfare that her freshly reupholstered—thanks to Miss Joan—car was finally ready to go.

The same could be said of Tina. Dr. Baker had released her sister from the hospital the night before, saying, oddly enough with the same sort of pleasure that Mick had displayed over the repaired vehicle, that Tina had made wonderful progress and that a full recovery was absolutely in her future.

Everything, it seemed to Olivia, was ready to go. Except for her.

At odds with her usual logical self, Olivia wanted to stay in Forever a little while longer. Stay, even though it wasn't practical or really possible. Her life, her work, her apartment, they were all back in Dallas. Harris Norvil had called her and said, because of the season, all was forgiven if she would return. He was giving her a last chance and she would be a fool not to snap it up.

There was nothing here in Forever for her. Nothing

except for a sheriff with hypnotic eyes and a mouth that drove her absolutely wild.

But that same mouth was not uttering words she needed to hear now. Packed and seemingly ready to depart, she was stalling, thanking Rick for his hospitality and for being so supportive during this whole ordeal. She was giving him every opportunity to say something, to "talk" her into staying even a week longer.

But Rick wasn't saying anything of the kind. He'd been silent throughout her entire little speech, as if he couldn't wait for her to be finished so he could get on with his day. Get on with his life.

And it was killing her.

Say something, damn it, she pleaded silently. *Tell me you want me to stay. Miss Joan told me you need a lawyer in Forever, but you never said anything about that, about my filling that slot. Or filling a place in your life. You didn't even say anything about my coming back for Christmas. Was everything just in my head?*

They stood there, almost like two strangers, with her making inept, awkward small talk. Two strangers instead of two lovers who had come to life in each other's arms, born again in each other's kisses.

Maybe it hadn't meant to him what it did to her. Olivia tried to shut out the ache and be philosophical about the way life turned out.

With a final, precise movement, she snapped the locks shut and put the suitcase on the floor beside the bed. She couldn't stall any longer.

"Listen," she said with forced brightness, "if you're ever in Dallas, just look me up. You'll have a place to stay."

"I'll keep that in mind," he replied stiffly.

He'd decided to turn down the interview for the position on the police force, but now he was having second thoughts about his second thoughts. Making up his mind one way or another required calm, quiet reflection, which he wasn't up to right now. His mind felt as if it was the center of a class-five hurricane, the antithesis of calm and quiet.

There was nothing left to do but walk her out. Picking up Olivia's suitcase, he carried it to the car for her. His gut was so utterly tied up in a knot, he felt like throwing up.

Rick turned from the car to see Olivia come out with Bobby in her arms and her sister walking slowly beside her.

He crossed to Tina and took her arm, threading it through his in order to give her the support she needed. Tina smiled her gratitude. In the few short days she'd spent here, she had come to like this tall, dark, handsome and somewhat stoic sheriff a great deal.

"Thank you for everything," Tina said as he opened the passenger door for her. She sank down on the seat, weary from the short trip she'd just taken. "And thank you for being so understanding about Bobby."

She knew without being told specifics that some other law enforcement officer might have turned the baby over to child services. That was still better by far than what Don had had in mind for the boy, but getting Bobby back would have meant going through hell.

"Just doing my job," Rick murmured, then realized how often he'd heard himself saying that these last couple of weeks or so.

He glanced over the roof of the vehicle. Olivia had just finished securing the baby in his infant seat and was turning toward the front of the car. Their eyes met and held. He felt his insides twisting again.

Damn it, stay woman. I can't ask you to give up everything for me. I don't have the right. But if you just said you wanted to stay, or at least that you didn't want to leave just yet, then I could tell you what I'm feeling. That I want you here with me.

But he remained silent.

Olivia saw the expression in his eyes, one she couldn't quite fathom. "Do you want to say something?" she asked, mentally crossing her fingers.

He wasn't conscious of the careless shrug that he gave, but she was.

"Just that I hope you have a safe trip." He held the door open for her and she got in, sitting behind the steering wheel. "You've got my number in case you run into trouble between here and Dallas."

She slid the seat belt tongue into the slot. "And what, you'll come riding to the rescue?"

He laughed shortly. There was no humor in the sound. "More like driving to the rescue and hey, it's the Texas way."

She nodded. This was pure torture. "We'll be fine." *If I don't break down and cry.* She looked at Tina, who was already strapped in. "Let's get you home, Tina."

Her sister breathed a sigh of relief. A look of tranquility seemed to come over her features. "Sounds good to me."

Olivia forced herself to smile as she started up the vehicle. "Yes, me, too."

Those were the last words he heard the woman who had his heart packed up in her suitcase say as he stepped back to let her leave.

He watched her drive away until the car was nothing more than a speck against the horizon, then remained there a little longer.

"How long will you go on being a jackass?"

The question came from Miss Joan as she poured a particularly inky cup of coffee for him. Rick had come in on his evening break, as he had been doing almost every evening ever since he'd become sheriff of this town. But, unlike all those other times, there was a heaviness to his step, a preoccupation about the expression on his face. Just as there had been for the past five days. Ever since that girl and her sister had left.

About to take a sip of the piping hot brew, he gazed up at the older woman. "What?"

Penciled-in dark brown eyebrows furrowed as she regarded Rick. She'd known him, man and boy, and prided herself on being able to read him better than he read himself. "You heard me. How much longer are you going to go on being a jackass?"

His took a sip, then another, before placing the cup back down on the counter. "Anything in particular you referring to?"

"Don't play games with me, boy," she warned sternly. "You know you want to go up there and see her. Be with her. Why don't you take that job offer that's been twisting in the wind and get on with your life?"

He'd only mentioned the possibility of going to Dallas for an interview. He hadn't said anything about the job actually being offered to him. "Anything you don't know, Miss Joan?"

"If that ever happens, you'll be the first to know," she promised, her expression the last word in drop-dead serious. Folding her hands together, she leaned over the counter and closer to him. "You know you're miserable without her. Anyone looking at you can see that. That friend of yours, Sam-something, he can get you on the force. You can go on being a law enforcement officer and still get the girl." She straightened up again, picking up her ever-present white cotton cloth and began polishing the counter. "If that's not the American dream, I don't know what is."

He didn't want to talk about it, not seriously. Not yet. He took another sip. "If I left, where would I get coffee like this?"

The cup was empty. She didn't refill it as was her habit. "I'll send you an urnful every Monday. Now quit talking and start packing."

He felt himself really vacillating. "I thought you liked having me around."

"I do. Only thing I like better is seeing you happy, not moping around all day with a hangdog expression on your face. Now, go." She punctuated her order by waving him on.

He circled the empty cup with his hands, staring down into it. "I'm thinking on it," was all he was willing to say at the moment.

"Think faster," she ordered as she went to tend to the customer who had just entered.

"It's his, isn't it?" Tina asked abruptly.

The question had come out of the blue, in the middle

of an inane conversation about the actual order of the articles cited in "The Twelve Days of Christmas."

Olivia stopped pretending that she had the slightest interest in decorating the tree she'd finally bought. Putting down her ornament, she turned to look at her sister. A nervousness undulated through her.

"Is what whose?"

Kindness and understanding flared in Tina's eyes. She was a far cry from the young woman who had stormed out of the apartment a short month ago. "The baby."

"You mean Bobby?" Olivia asked innocently, turning away. "You said that—"

Tina moved so that she was in front of her sister again. "You know, for a clever lawyer, you throw up a very poor smoke screen." She shook her head, but there was no judgment in her eyes. "No, not Bobby. I heard you throwing up this morning. And the morning before that. And the morning before that," she enumerated. Just a shade taller than her sister, she put her hand comfortingly on Olivia's shoulder. "I've been through this, Livy. Except that you, luckily, have a much nicer guy as the baby's father."

Where had this sudden urge to cry come from? She felt it scratching at her throat, trying to burst free. It took her a second to get it under control.

"I don't *have* anything," Olivia corrected her sister. "In all likelihood, I'll never see the man again." And just saying that hurt. Hurt like hell.

Tina had a simple solution. "You would if you went back down there."

Olivia stared at her, dumbfounded. "Just pop up? Tina, I can't go and—"

"No, not pop up," Tina contradicted. "I'm talking about going back there to live."

This time, Olivia laughed. The situation was far from funny, but Tina's simplistic take on it was. "Oh, even better. And just what would my excuse be?" she asked, then answered her own question. "You want me to walk up to Rick and say, 'Excuse me, Sheriff, but I believe I have something of yours? Some of your genes accidentally mingled with mine and it appears that I'm having your baby'?" She forced herself to pick up another ornament. "That, my dear, is a conversation stopper, not a conversation starter."

Tina took the ornament out of her hand and put it down. She bracketed Olivia's shoulders with her hands and looked into her eyes. "He deserves to know, Livy."

Olivia shook her head and shrugged out of Tina's hold. "Trust me, he'll be happier not knowing."

Tina picked up on the lead-in Olivia had given her. "Speaking of happy, you haven't been happy since we came back."

Olivia shrugged as she circled the tree, looking for the right place to hang the ornament she'd retrieved for a second time. "I've had a lot of work to catch up on. Nobody took up the slack while I was gone."

Tina saw through the flimsy excuse. "It's not the work and you know it." She glanced over her shoulder toward the room where Bobby was sleeping. "Why don't we just pack up and go back?"

That stopped Olivia in her tracks. It never occurred

to her that Tina would ever want to see that region of the state again.

"We? You mean you and Bobby, too? You actually want to move to Forever?"

Just a short while ago, the Tina she knew would have made some kind of snide remark about not being caught dead in a place where they rolled up the sidewalks after ten o'clock at night. This was quite a change—if she actually meant it.

But there was no indication that her sister was joking or pulling her leg. Tina looked—and sounded—sincere.

"It seems like a really nice, safe place to raise a kid. There're just bad memories for me here, Livy," she confessed. "I could start fresh there." Tina's eyes met hers. "Do it for Bobby and me if not for you."

"Like I don't see through that." Even so, she would have been willing to give it a try if not for one thing. "If Rick had given me the slightest indication that he wanted me to stay, maybe I could go back. But he didn't. He's probably forgotten all about me by now."

Tina stared at her incredulously. "In a week?"

"You'd be surprised how quickly men can develop amnesia—" The doorbell rang just then and she sighed. She was doing a lot of that lately. Sighing and throwing up and feeling as if her hormones were in the middle of a fierce tennis match. "That'll be the pizza I ordered. Could you do me a favor and get the door?"

"Sure." Tina left the room. A minute later, Olivia heard her sister opening the door. And then Tina called out, "It's not the pizza delivery guy, Liv."

The closer it got to Christmas, the more the local kids tried to hawk cards and wrapping paper and cookies even ants weren't interested in. She'd already bought more than her share. "Then tell whoever it is we don't want whatever they're selling."

"Don't you want to hear me out, first?"

The glass ornament slipped from her fingers, hitting the rug and rolling toward the base of the tree. Olivia turned from the eight-foot fir, her heart already pounding madly even as she told herself she was just imagining his voice.

But it wasn't her imagination.

Her mouth went dry.

He was standing in her living room, a black Stetson on his head, a tanned sheepskin jacket and worn jeans on his body and even more worn boots on his feet. All that was missing was the star.

"Rick."

He took off his hat and held it in his hands. If she didn't know better, she would have said he looked nervous. "Hi."

She blinked once. He was still there. "What are you doing here?"

"Feeling damn awkward," he admitted freely. "But it seemed like a good idea at the time."

Her brain felt as if it had gone into a deep freeze. "What did?"

Rick took a deep breath. "Coming here to tell you that I'm going to take a job with the Dallas police force."

Tina came to life. "I think I hear Bobby waking up," she announced. "I'll just go and look in on him." She paused to grin at the father of her sister's baby. "So great seeing you again, Rick," she told him, then gave him a quick kiss on the cheek before all but flying out of the room.

Rick ran the brim of his hat through his fingers. "She looks good," he commented.

"She is." They'd gone to see the doctor that Dr. Baker had recommended and he'd had nothing but encouraging words to say about Tina's obvious progress. "Getting stronger every day. But she can't act worth a damn." Olivia turned her attention back to him. Her heart pounded harder. He couldn't be saying what she thought she heard him saying. "So, you're really moving here?"

He nodded. "Seems like the thing to do. The commute would be a bear otherwise."

He had to be kidding. Didn't he? *Oh, please let him be kidding.* "Oh. That's too bad."

He thought she'd be happy that he was coming to Dallas. Had he misread the signs? "Why?" he asked cautiously.

She watched Rick's face carefully as she said, "Because Tina and I were just talking about moving to Forever."

Suddenly he was feeling a whole lot better. "You were? Why?"

She gave him Tina's reason, not her own. "Seems like a good place to raise a child. While we were there, there was definitely a feeling that everyone was looking out for Bobby. That wouldn't happen in Dallas. People don't take an interest in one another the way they do in Forever."

"It's a great place," he agreed enthusiastically. But he

needed to be absolutely sure before he let his happiness loose. "You're really serious?"

Was it her imagination, or were the lights on the tree suddenly glowing brighter? "I'm really serious."

His sigh of relief was huge. "Then I don't have to take that job on the Dallas PD and move here."

She needed more. She needed to have him spell things out. "Why would you *have to?*"

He looked at her as if she should know the answer to that. "To be near you."

She heard him, but she was reluctant to allow herself to believe what he was saying. Because she wanted it too much. "You'd give up everything to be near me?"

"Don't you get it, Livy? You *are* everything," he told her in a quiet, firm voice. Stepping forward, he opened his jacket and enfolded her in his arms. Next to his heart. "Are you prepared to make an honest man of me?"

She felt warm and safe and sheltered. Olivia lifted her head to look up at him. "Isn't it usually the other way around?"

"Times have changed," he informed her. "This is called equality." The smile on his lips faded as he watched her in earnest. "I know this is short notice, but it feels as if I've been waiting for you for a long, long time. I love you, Olivia." And then he set her world on its ear by asking, "Will you marry me?"

She felt like laughing and crying, all at the same time. She wanted to shout yes, but not before everything was out on the table.

Olivia pressed her lips together, then said, "You have to know something first."

He braced himself. Whatever it was, it didn't matter.

He'd handle it. As long as she was his in the end. "There's someone else?"

"In a way." She took a breath, but it didn't help. Taking a thousand breaths wouldn't make saying this any easier. "I'm pregnant." She saw him grow very still. Oh God, she'd lost him before she ever had him. "I don't know how, we did all the right things, but there you have it. I'm pregnant and the baby is yours."

"How long have you known?" he asked her quietly.

She was right, she'd lost him. Who wanted to have an instant family when he got married? "A week."

"Why didn't you call me?" His voice grew in volume. She still couldn't tell if he was angry about the baby—or excited. But she knew which side she was rooting for.

At first, she'd been tempted to call, but her more practical side had prevailed. "Because I know the kind of man you are and I didn't want you to feel you *had* to marry me."

His features softened, and she knew everything was going to be all right. "Now there you're wrong. I do have to marry you—because the thought of someone else holding either you or our baby would kill me. Now you have to say yes," he told her. "You'd be saving my life."

Olivia found herself back to the laughing/crying reaction again. She felt wonderful. "You are a crazy person, you know that?"

"You're stalling."

"Yes," she declared. "Yes, I love you. Yes, I'll marry you." She threaded her arms around his neck. Everything inside of her felt like singing. "Every day of the week, if you want."

"Just one day will be fine," he assured her. "Oh, wait." Pausing, he dug into the pocket of his sheepskin jacket. "Miss Joan gave me this mistletoe twig for luck, in case I needed help to get you to kiss me." He held it up over her head.

"You don't need a mistletoe for luck—or to get me to kiss you. But I'd better do it now before I decide this is all a dream, because I've been dying inside ever since I watched you disappear in my rearview mirror."

Tossing the mistletoe aside, he closed the sides of his jacket around her again, absorbing the heat of her body into his own. He couldn't remember the last time he'd felt this happy. Except with her. "Looks like we're going to have a merry Christmas after all."

Olivia turned her face up to his. "My thoughts, exactly."

They were the last thoughts she had for a very long while. Thinking would have only gotten in the way of what happened next.

* * * * *

Look out for the next book in
Marie Ferrarella's Forever, Texas, miniseries,
RAMONA AND THE RENEGADE.

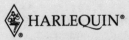

COMING NEXT MONTH

Available December 7, 2010

#1333 HER CHRISTMAS HERO
Babies & Bachelors USA
Linda Warren

#1334 A COWBOY UNDER THE MISTLETOE
Texas Legacies: The McCabes
Cathy Gillen Thacker

#1335 THE HOLIDAY TRIPLETS
Safe Harbor Medical
Jacqueline Diamond

#1336 THE BULL RIDER'S CHRISTMAS BABY
The Buckhorn Ranch
Laura Marie Altom

REQUEST YOUR FREE BOOKS!
2 FREE NOVELS PLUS 2 FREE GIFTS!

HARLEQUIN®
American Romance®

Love, Home & Happiness!

YES! Please send me 2 FREE Harlequin® American Romance® novels and my 2 FREE gifts (gifts are worth about $10). After receiving them, if I don't wish to receive any more books, I can return the shipping statement marked "cancel." If I don't cancel, I will receive 4 brand-new novels every month and be billed just $4.24 per book in the U.S. or $4.99 per book in Canada. That's a saving of at least 15% off the cover price! It's quite a bargain! Shipping and handling is just 50¢ per book.* I understand that accepting the 2 free books and gifts places me under no obligation to buy anything. I can always return a shipment and cancel at any time. Even if I never buy another book from Harlequin, the two free books and gifts are mine to keep forever.

154/354 HDN E5LG

Name _____ (PLEASE PRINT)

Address _____ Apt. #

City _____ State/Prov. _____ Zip/Postal Code

Signature (if under 18, a parent or guardian must sign)

Mail to the **Harlequin Reader Service:**
IN U.S.A.: P.O. Box 1867, Buffalo, NY 14240-1867
IN CANADA: P.O. Box 609, Fort Erie, Ontario L2A 5X3

Not valid for current subscribers to Harlequin® American Romance® books.

Want to try two free books from another line?
Call 1-800-873-8635 or visit www.morefreebooks.com.

* Terms and prices subject to change without notice. Prices do not include applicable taxes. N.Y. residents add applicable sales tax. Canadian residents will be charged applicable provincial taxes and GST. Offer not valid in Quebec. This offer is limited to one order per household. All orders subject to approval. Credit or debit balances in a customer's account(s) may be offset by any other outstanding balance owed by or to the customer. Please allow 4 to 6 weeks for delivery. Offer available while quantities last.

Your Privacy: Harlequin is committed to protecting your privacy. Our Privacy Policy is available online at www.eHarlequin.com or upon request from the Reader Service. From time to time we make our lists of customers available to reputable third parties who may have a product or service of interest to you. If you would prefer we not share your name and address, please check here. ☐

Help us get it right—We strive for accurate, respectful and relevant communications. To clarify or modify your communication preferences, visit us at www.ReaderService.com/consumerchoice.

HAR10R

HARLEQUIN®

A Romance

FOR EVERY MOOD™

Spotlight on

Classic

Quintessential, modern love stories
that are romance at its finest.

See the next page
to enjoy a sneak peek from
the Harlequin® Romance series.

See below for a sneak peek from our classic
Harlequin® Romance® line.

Introducing DADDY BY CHRISTMAS by Patricia Thayer.

MIA caught sight of Jarrett when he walked into the open lobby. It was hard not to notice the man. In a charcoal business suit with a crisp white shirt and striped tie covered by a dark trench coat, he looked more Wall Street than small-town Colorado.

Mia couldn't blame him for keeping his distance. He was probably tired of taking care of her.

Besides, why would a man like Jarrett McKane be interested in her? Why would he want to take on a woman expecting a baby? Yet he'd done so many things for her. He'd been there when she'd needed him most. How could she not care about a man like that?

Heart pounding in her ears, she walked up behind him. Jarrett turned to face her. "Did you get enough sleep last night?"

"Yes, thanks to you," she said, wondering if he'd thought about their kiss. Her gaze went to his mouth, then she quickly glanced away. "And thank you for not bringing up my meltdown."

Jarrett couldn't stop looking at Mia. Blue was definitely her color, bringing out the richness of her eyes.

"What meltdown?" he said, trying hard to focus on what she was saying. "You were just exhausted from lack of sleep and worried about your baby."

He couldn't help remembering how, during the night, he'd kept going in to watch her sleep. How strange was that? "I hope you got enough rest."

She nodded. "Plenty. And you're a good neighbor for

coming to my rescue."

He tensed. Neighbor? *What neighbor kisses you like I did?* "That's me, just the full-service landlord," he said, trying to keep the sarcasm out of his voice. He started to leave, but she put her hand on his arm.

"Jarrett, what I meant was you went beyond helping me." Her eyes searched his face. "I've asked far too much of you."

"Did you hear me complain?"

She shook her head. "You should. I feel like I've taken advantage."

"Like I said, I haven't minded."

"And I'm grateful for everything…"

Grasping her hand on his arm, Jarrett leaned forward. The memory of last night's kiss had him aching for another. "I didn't do it for your gratitude, Mia."

Gorgeous tycoon Jarrett McKane has never believed in Christmas—but he can't help being drawn to soon-to-be-mom Mia Saunders! Christmases past were spent alone…and now Jarrett may just have a fairy-tale ending for all his Christmases future!

Available December 2010, only from Harlequin® Romance®.

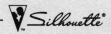

SPECIAL EDITION

USA TODAY BESTSELLING AUTHOR

MARIE FERRARELLA

**BRINGS YOU ANOTHER
HEARTWARMING STORY FROM**

When Lilli McCall disappeared on him
after he proposed, Kullen Manetti swore
never to fall in love again. Eight years later
Lilli is back in his life, threatening to break
down all the walls he's put up to
safeguard his heart.

UNWRAPPING
THE PLAYBOY

*Available December
wherever books are sold.*

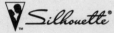
Silhouette®

ROMANTIC
SUSPENSE
Sparked by Danger, Fueled by Passion.

RACHEL LEE
A Soldier's Redemption

When the Witness Protection Program fails at keeping Cory Farland out of harm's way, ex-marine Wade Kendrick steps in. As Cory's new bodyguard, Wade has a plan for protecting her—however falling in love was not part of his plan.

Conard County *THE NEXT GENERATION*

Available in December wherever books are sold.

Visit Silhouette Books at www.eHarlequin.com

SRS27705